# HIS PROMISE

**Also by Shelley Shepard Gray**

*Sisters of the Heart series*
HIDDEN • WANTED • FORGIVEN • GRACE

*Seasons of Sugarcreek series*
WINTER'S AWAKENING
SPRING'S RENEWAL
AUTUMN'S PROMISE
CHRISTMAS IN SUGARCREEK

*Families of Honor series*
THE CAREGIVER
THE PROTECTOR
THE SURVIVOR
A CHRISTMAS FOR KATIE (novella)

*The Secrets of Crittenden County series*
MISSING • THE SEARCH • FOUND • PEACE

*The Days of Redemption series*
DAYBREAK
RAY OF LIGHT
EVENTIDE
SNOWFALL

*Return to Sugarcreek series*
HOPEFUL
THANKFUL
JOYFUL

*Amish Brides of Pinecraft series*
THE PROMISE OF PALM GROVE
THE PROPOSAL AT SIESTA KEY
A WEDDING AT THE ORANGE BLOSSOM INN
A WISH ON GARDENIA STREET (novella)
A CHRISTMAS BRIDE IN PINECRAFT

*The Charmed Amish Life series*
A SON'S VOW
A DAUGHTER'S DREAM
A SISTER'S WISH
AN AMISH FAMILY CHRISTMAS

*The Amish of Hart County series*
HER SECRET
HIS GUILT
THE GIFT
HIS RISK
HER FEAR

# HIS PROMISE

## AN AMISH CHRISTMAS IN HART COUNTY

# Shelley Shepard Gray

AVON

**INSPIRE**

*An Imprint of HarperCollinsPublishers*

First Avon Inspire mass market printing: November 2018
First Avon Inspire hardcover printing: October 2018

Print Edition ISBN: 978-0-06-286932-6
Digital Edition ISBN: 978-0-06-246920-5

FIRST EDITION

18 19 20 21 22 LSC 10 9 8 7 6 5 4 3 2 1

*For everyone who loves dogs,*
*especially tiny, opinionated dachshunds.*

# ACKNOWLEDGMENTS

I owe a world of gratitude to the folks at Avon for both the idea and the production of the Amish of Hart County series. Writing six books over two years that were suspenseful yet not exactly a series was a bit of a challenge for me! I couldn't have done it without the direction of my incredible editorial team of Erika Tsang, Nicole Fischer, Patrice Silverstein, and Julia Meltzer. Each of them was integral in making sure every book was the best it could be. And the covers! I loved how fresh and different each one was from my previous novels. I wish all authors were as blessed as I have been to have such a great team of people by their side.

I'm indebted to my critique partners, especially Heather Blake Webber, Lynne Stroup, my first reader, and to my Amish friends who gave the books their stamp of approval, even though some of my characters did very bad things. I'm also thankful to my street team, the Buggy Bunch, who read all the books and helped me spread the word about Hart County. Finally, I'm so grateful for the many librarians who have placed my books on their shelves, told their patrons about my books, and have even invited me to visit their towns. What a blessing!

This note wouldn't be complete without a word of thanks to my readers. When I made the scary decision to write my first Amish novel, I had no idea that this choice would lead me on such an incredible journey that would last over a decade. Even more special have been the many reader friends I've made, both online and in person. Just thinking about y'all makes my heart full. Thank you for your support, your faith, and your kindness.

I will be filled with joy because of You. I will sing praises to your name, O Most High.

PSALM 9:2

Prayers go up, Blessings come down.

AMISH PROVERB

# HIS PROMISE

# CHAPTER 1

It's snowing again," Grace King said to Snooze. "If it keeps up, we're gonna have a white Christmas. Won't that be something?"

Snooze, the five-year-old dachshund who hadn't been named by accident, opened one eye, stared at her for a few seconds, then darted under his favorite quilt. Grace knew he wouldn't reappear for several hours.

He was truly the most unsocial animal she'd ever cared for, and that was saying a lot. She'd taken care of a variety of animals during her three years as a professional pet sitter. From pampered felines to retired greyhounds to ornery parrots, she'd sat for them all. Grace even once watched a high school science teacher's iguana named Sam. With every animal, she'd managed to find something to connect with. Sometimes, all it took was a special treat or a couple of games of fetch. Or, in Sam's case, fresh crickets.

Snooze, all fourteen pounds of stubbornness, was starting to be her most difficult charge. No matter what she did, the little wire-haired dachshund didn't want anything to do with her. It was frustrating, but at least she knew the reason.

Snooze was pouting.

He missed his family and was extremely displeased that he was having to spend Christmas with her. *Only* her.

Grace knew exactly how he felt.

It wasn't supposed to be this way. When Mr. and Mrs. Lee booked her services back in September, they'd kindly told Grace that she should feel free to have any of her siblings or one of her girlfriends keep her company while she lived in their big house for two weeks.

Imagining quiet evenings spent on their soft leather couches in front of their fireplace with her best friend, Jennifer, or one of her sisters, Grace jumped at the chance. She was the second oldest of six children—and while she loved, loved, loved them all, she was also the quietest of the King family.

They were a noisy and gregarious lot. They were easily excited, had definite opinions about everything, and were constantly in each other's business. Grace sometimes found them to be overwhelming.

No, that wasn't quite true. The truth was that she found them to be overwhelming most of the time. She wasn't exactly sure why God had given her a quiet demeanor in the midst of such a rambunctious crowd, but He had.

Usually, she took her family's boisterousness in stride, but at Christmas everything just seemed to get worse.

Christmas at their house was anything but plain and simple. Though they didn't have a tree or strung lights from the roof, her mother would hang Christmas cards down the banisters, light cranberry-scented candles from morning till night, and even sing Christmas carols to herself when she didn't think anyone was listening. And then there was the baking. And the wrapping. And the dozen holiday projects in various stages of completion scattered all through the house.

It was a little bit chaotic for someone like Grace, who enjoyed the quiet almost as much as she enjoyed being alone with a good book.

Grace had planned to use the Lees' beautiful, roomy, quiet house as her Christmas escape. She'd planned to attach Snooze's leash to his collar and take him home for a few hours every day so everyone could play with him. Then, when they were both tired, she'd usher him back to his fancy house, where they could revel in the peace and quiet.

But almost as soon as she'd said good-bye to Mr. and Mrs.

Lee—*and* got snubbed by Snooze—the Lord rearranged her plans: Mamm's parents contracted a bad case of the flu, and were so weak that the whole family—well, everyone except her—journeyed up to Ohio to spend the holiday at Mommi's and Dawdi's *haus*.

Then Jennifer *and* her family decided to travel for the holiday as well.

Now, to make matters worse, Grace's *only* companion had turned out to be an unsocial dachshund who would rather sleep under an old quilt than spend time with her.

She was feeling a little blue, and restless, too. None of the books she'd brought with her caught her interest. Neither did the puzzle she'd placed on the kitchen table.

It seemed she was pouting, too.

After staring out the window again, then surveying the sparkling clean and far-too quiet room, Grace came to a decision. She needed to stop feeling sorry for herself. It was only day two of her fifteen-day job. Something had to be done.

"Snooze, let's go for a little walk."

The dog stuck out its tiny brown nose.

"I see you thinking about it. Come on. It will be fun."

Snooze grumbled when she scooped him up into her arms, but didn't try to wriggle free. Feeling encouraged, Grace clipped a leash to his collar and set him back down. Then she threw a scarf around her neck, stuffed her feet into boots she'd neatly placed by the door, grabbed her black cloak, and led Snooze outside.

After closing the shiny black door behind her, she sighed in pleasure. The Lees' front yard was a winter wonderland . . . rolling hills covered in white, clumps of trees and bushes arranged in artful arrangements, a lovely walkway meandering over to the side of the house, and bright-red cardinals perched on a black wrought-iron feeder. A couple of squirrels were chattering in the distance. It all looked and felt like something out of a Christmas card.

"You surely have quite a home, Snooze," she murmured.

When the little dog squirmed, she smiled. *"Jah,* I bet you are ready to do your business." Kneeling, she unclipped the leash so he could wander around the yard and sniff. She'd already learned that Snooze's bathroom breaks never took too long. Usually after less than five minutes, he would be at her side, ready to get picked up and transported back into the house. Snooze didn't seem to like getting his paws snowy.

Just as he'd done every time before, Snooze gingerly walked a few steps, sniffed the ground. Circled, sniffed a holly bush. Paused. The squirrels in the distance chattered again. He raised his head toward them.

Then, in a startling, lightning-fast move, he barked shrilly and took off running down a hill.

Before she could react, he was out of sight.

"Snooze? Snooze!" Feeling an odd combination of both shock and panic, Grace ran after him, the hem of her dark-green dress and apron brushing against the snow and soaking her stocking-covered legs.

"Snooze! Come back!" Down the hill she went, following tiny footprints like a detective. Frantically calling out his name.

But he didn't come.

Twenty yards into her run, she stopped gripping her cloak. And because she'd never fastened it, it slid off her shoulders. She left it on the ground, too afraid to look anywhere but at the paw prints in the snow. "Snooze! Snooze, come here, wouldja?"

But still there was no answer.

And then, to her dismay, there were no more tracks to be found. She could only surmise that he'd gone after one of those pesky squirrels into the woods, where the ground was covered with more mud and pine needles than snow.

Standing there in the cold, her fingertips beginning to feel like ice, her cloak lying on the ground, and her head bare except for her white *kapp*, Grace forced herself to face the awful, awful truth.

She'd just managed to lose her only companion—and her only responsibility—for the holiday.

"Snooze!" she yelled out again. "Please, please come back!"

Tears filled her eyes as she stepped forward. She was going to have to start wandering through the woods, all while praying that some fox or other wild animal hadn't taken hold of the dog.

"Snooze!" Her feet crunched on the blanket of frozen mud and pine needles. She reached out and moved a branch out of her path, really wishing she'd put on mittens.

Squirrels scampered overhead, a hawk circled in the distance. Just as she pulled another branch out of her way, another scraped her cheek.

The snow continued to fall, large flakes sticking to the branches surrounding her, clinging to her wool dress.

And still, there was no sign of the dog.

The tears that she'd tried to quell began trickling down her face. "Snooze? Here, pup."

She stopped again. She was now surrounded by trees and had no idea which way to go. No idea how to tempt one disagreeable dachshund to return to her side.

Just as she was about to call his name again, she heard a loud rustling off to her left.

With a cry of relief, she turned toward the noise. Then screamed as a man broke through a tangle of branches and rushed toward her.

# CHAPTER 2

Just as Grace screamed again, the man raised his hands in surrender. "Hey, it's okay!" he called out, lumbering through the woods like a bulldozer. "I heard you call out. Is Snooze—*Wait*, is that you, Grace?"

Stunned that he'd spoken her name, Grace inhaled sharply, the frigid air burning her lungs. Gathering herself together, she eyed the Amish man dressed in a black stocking cap, black wool coat, and dark-blue pants. He could have been anyone . . . until she noticed his eyes.

The very same light-brown eyes fringed with thick eyelashes that used to haunt her dreams. "John Michael Miller?" she asked at last, hardly able to believe it. Could it really be her sister Beth's former boyfriend standing right in front of her?

"*Jah*. It's me." His voice softened as he hurried toward her.

While she stood there, half shaking from both the cold and the shock, he reached out and rubbed his gloved hands along her arms. "Grace, where is your coat? You must be freezing! And what are you doing out here in the woods?"

He looked down at her with concern, his burly, tall body practically looming over her own slight frame.

"I've lost Mr. and Mrs. Lee's dog. Will you help me, John Michael?"

"*Jah*. Of course. This has happened before."

"How do you know?"

"I live right next door, Silly," he replied. "Snooze is surely the cutest little dachshund I've ever seen . . . but, I fear, he's a bit of a handful, too."

*Silly.* That's what he'd called her when dating Beth almost three years ago. Though it was bitter cold out and snowflakes were sticking to her face and clothing, she felt herself heat up in embarrassment. That pet name brought up so many memories, most of them reminding her of just how awkward she used to be.

Fearing he'd spy her telltale blush, she turned to scan the fields. "Where has Snooze gone in the past?"

"He likes to chase the squirrels, then gets tired quickly. We usually find him near my compost pile."

This adventure was getting worse and worse. Now, if she did find the little dachshund, there was a mighty good chance he was going to be smelly and in need of a bath. "Which way is that?"

"I'll take you. But first, let's get you warm."

It took her a moment to register that he was taking off his wool coat and intending for her to wear it. "I don't need your coat."

"*Jah.* You do." He held it up. "You're freezing. Let me help you."

She *was* freezing. And the snow was still coming down, beginning to soak through her dress. "All right," she said as she slid her arms into the sinfully warm sleeves, thinking that she should offer to give it back. But even without the coat, he was dressed far more appropriately for the weather than she was.

Grace pushed the coat sleeves up just far enough to be able to fasten two of the buttons and glanced at him. "It's toasty warm. I feel better already."

"I bet it's warm. It looks like it's trying to swallow you whole." He chuckled. "Looks like my arms are still longer than yours. Give me an arm."

She held out one and silently watched him roll the sleeves. Now she'd be able to pick up Snooze when and if they ever found him.

"*Danke,*" she said after he rolled up the second sleeve.

"It's nothing." Looking far more serious, he inhaled. "Grace, maybe we should talk about—"

"*Snooze*," she said firmly. "We need to locate that *hund* before he either gets eaten by a wild animal or freezes to death."

His eyes lit up. "Looks like your imagination is alive and well. Come on, then. Follow me."

When he turned around and started going back in the direction from which he came, she followed in his footsteps. As she trailed behind him, staring at his back in a mixture of relief, hope, and confusion, Grace couldn't help but remember how things used to be.

Like many other Amish families in the county, the Millers had come from up north. Back when she was still a teenager, she'd thought Bird-in-Hand, Pennsylvania, sounded almost cosmopolitan. And in her naiveté, eighteen-year-old John Michael was everything she, and most of the residents of Horse Cave, Kentucky, were not. He had an air about him that was both worldly and mature. That attitude, combined with his dark-brown hair and brown eyes, had set just about every Amish teenaged girl's heart in the county to go a-patter.

Her sister Beth had been no exception. From practically the first moment she'd seen John Michael, she was smitten.

But for nine months, their parents encouraged them to take things slow. Every Sunday, whether they were attending church at someone's house or it was an off week, John Michael would come over for Sunday supper.

Beth would beam at him and generally act like he was an honored guest. To Grace's shame, Beth wasn't the only one. Grace had to try hard to quell her own crush, but wasn't able to entirely hide her feelings. He started calling her "Silly" and treating her like a lost child. She was sixteen at the time, yet sure she was mature and grown up. His pet name had stung badly.

Then, just when Beth was sure they were going to become engaged, John Michael abruptly broke things off. And followed, in a move no one in her family could understand, with volunteering for the Hart County Fire Department. They had *never* heard him say anything about the fire department. They'd all assumed he was going to take over his parents' farm.

"You okay back there, Grace?" he called out. "You're being mighty quiet."

Though she ached to tell him she wasn't a chattering little girl anymore, that she was almost twenty, she answered simply. "I am fine."

"Ah." After another few seconds, he cleared his throat. "I know you're worried about Snooze, but I promise you that he is most likely fine. It's been my experience that animals have a better sense of direction than people. I imagine he'll find his way back by nightfall."

*Snooze!* Had he even crossed her mind during the last five minutes? No, he had not. What kind of terrible pet sitter had she become?

Getting her head back to the task at hand, she attempted to sound more hopeful than she felt. "I certainly hope so."

He stopped and turned around, concern etched across his features. "If he isn't lounging near the compost pile, I promise that I won't let you look for him alone."

"That is too kind of you."

"He's a sweet little guy. Of course I don't want him lost in a snowstorm. Or you, either."

The smile and concerned expression on his face was kind. Almost brotherly.

It was everything proper.

So why did it chafe so much?

Smiling slightly, he added, "And of course, I'm not going to let you shoulder this burden alone. How did you come to be looking after him anyway?"

"I am a pet sitter. It's my job."

"You are? Since when?"

She hated how he sounded, like she was a little girl trying on her mother's clothes. Though it was prideful, she lifted her chin.

"Since three years ago."

"Really? You've been working all this time?" he asked as he took care to walk by her side. "That would have been, what? When you were seventeen?"

"Sixteen."

"How old are you now? Eighteen?"

"I'm nineteen. Nearly twenty." Almost as soon as she said the words, she wished she could take them back. She sounded so full of herself.

But John Michael only looked amused. His lips twitched. "You're right. I still remember that your birthday is right near Jesus's. Just a few weeks after, yes?"

"*Jah*. January 14." Before she realized she was doing it, Grace lifted her chin again, like she had something special to prove. When she noticed that he noticed her slight movement, she blushed.

Oh, but he had an awful way of making her feel ridiculous. "Are we close, John Michael?"

"Hmm? Oh, *jah*. Just a little bit farther."

She looked around, eyeing the rolling hills, the brown trees lying dormant until spring, the frozen creek bed. It was a lovely farm. "I don't remember your family having so much land. I guess I didn't think about things like that when I was younger."

"I doubt you worried about acreage, but your memory isn't wrong. We didn't have as much land until Miss Schultz sold her farm."

The name rang a bell . . . though, she and her sisters had always called her Miss Dorma. On its heels rode in sweet memories of a kind lady who baked up a storm, and always had some kind of toffee or taffy in her purse. Any child lucky enough to sit next to Miss Dorma during church would be given a treat to tide them over until the preacher finished his sermon.

In spite of the awkwardness of the situation, Grace smiled. "I haven't thought about Miss Dorma in years. She moved far away, didn't she?"

"I don't believe so. Last I heard, she was living with some distant relatives in town." His voice drifted off. "I'm a little ashamed to admit that I haven't thought about her in months."

"Next time I go to Bill's Diner, I'll ask about her. Maybe one of the servers has seen her or is part of her church district."

"That's a *gut* idea." His voice warmed. "No doubt she's still bringing treats to the *kinner* there." He pointed toward a pile of straw, food scraps, and what looked like shredded newspaper about six or seven yards away. "Snooze likes to nose around that." He held out a hand. "Come, I'll take you there."

She ignored his hand. "Snooze!" she called out, increasing her pace.

"Careful! Silly, the ground is a little uneven over there. It can be treacherous when it's covered in snow."

"I'm fine." Then, as if on cue, she stumbled and twisted her ankle. It stung, but she righted herself . . . just as she stumbled again.

"Grace, wait."

Whether it was because she was embarrassed or had finally decided to stop being so prideful, she did as he asked. But, boy, it was difficult to spy that familiar look of concern in his features. Was she ever going to be grown up and poised in his eyes?

He reached for her hand. "Are you okay?"

Unable to ignore his touch, she gripped his fingers. "*Jah. Danke.*"

Then, realizing what she was doing, she laughed softly. "I promise, I'm really not that clumsy anymore."

His hand floated back down to his side. "I don't remember you being clumsy in the first place," he murmured before continuing in a bright tone of voice. "Usually, Snooze is right . . . *here.*"

She hurried to a mound of straw and what looked to be the last of the fall leaves . . . and a pile of apple peels.

Nestled in the middle of it was a sleeping Snooze. "Thank you, Jesus!" she murmured as she carefully knelt down and scooped up the pup.

To her relief, the dog was warm and seemed fine. He didn't

appear sick or chilled, only sleepy. Snooze opened his eyes, sniffed her coat, then yawned.

"Oh, Snooze. Thank goodness you were here."

For the first time since she'd begun to watch him, the dog snuggled closer instead of stiffening and attempting to spring free.

It seemed that bit of trust was all her body needed to finally let down her guard. She hadn't lost him! He wasn't hurt. He was going to be just fine.

Tears in her eyes, she turned to John Michael. "I'm so grateful for your help. You saved the day!"

"I don't know about that."

"I do! If you hadn't found me, Snooze would still be alone, and I would be wandering in the woods by myself without even a coat on. Thank you so much for helping me."

"You're welcome." His voice sounded a little thick. He wasn't smiling now, either. Just looked at her intently.

Which made her heart beat a little faster.

Which was wrong.

Feeling more confused than ever, Grace backed up. "I should leave. I'm sure Snooze is ready to snuggle under his favorite quilt."

"There's a lot of snow on the ground now. How about you let me hitch up the sled? You'd get home much faster."

Gliding across the snowy hills next to John Michael? Sitting so close to him that their bodies would touch? All while wearing his coat?

That was a recipe for disaster. "*Danke,* but *nee.* My cloak fell off almost as soon as I started running. I need to retrieve it."

"I'll help you find it. There's no need to go alone."

*There's no need to go alone.* A shiver ran through her. Hadn't that been what she'd been trying to do, with rather poor results? "That is too kind of you. *Danke.*"

"Do you want to come inside my house for a few minutes first? I could make you some hot cider or tea."

No matter how cozy his coat was, her cheeks and nose were

chilled. Sipping a hot drink and resting her sore ankle for a moment sounded heavenly, as did taking a moment to relax.

However, being around John Michael after all this time was proving to be anything but relaxing. The sparks of desire that she'd so unsuccessfully tried to tamp down all those years ago had flared again. Embarrassing her. She knew she could never, ever be with the one man who'd broken her sister's heart. Beth would never forgive her.

And, maybe, she wouldn't be able to forgive herself?

There was only one decision. "I better not."

"You are in that big of a hurry to get home?"

She could lie and take the easy way out . . . but she wasn't going to do that anymore. "You know why I'm saying no, John. It's for the best."

"Is it?" Before she could figure out a way to remind him that any friendship between them would be difficult on account of her sister's feelings, he shook his head. "You know what? Forget it. Let's go, Grace."

She'd stood up for her sister. She was going her way, and she'd deftly sidestepped his offers and kindness. She should feel pretty good.

So why did she feel so awful about the new barrier that was between them?

Her mind a muddled mess, she followed him across the fields again, all the while wishing she could have handled their reunion a better way.

# CHAPTER 3

John Michael had hoped he would never be alone with Grace King again.

She made him feel too vulnerable. Too tentative, too not like himself. Though he was by nature reticent, there was something about her that made him feel like he was only a couple of minutes away from baring his soul and confessing his darkest secrets.

Thinking back to when he'd been courting her older sister, Beth, John Michael knew there were several times when he'd almost told her far too much.

All that was why for the last three years he'd kept a healthy distance from Grace King. It had been a challenge. They lived in a close-knit community. Practically every person of Amish faith knew everyone else. However, he'd become adept at avoiding any singings or gatherings where the King girls were going to be.

A lot of people probably had no idea he was keeping his distance. His mother and father were not among them. Over and over, they'd questioned his choices.

More than once his father had advised him to move on. He'd remind John that even though he'd hurt Beth, he was only human. He was going to make mistakes, he was going to change his mind, and he was going to need forgiveness at times, too. He also reminded John that dwelling on the past never did anyone much good.

All of his father's words made sense. But it didn't mean they were easy to put into practice.

Now, as he slowly walked beside Grace in the snow, John Michael was struck by two things. The first was that Grace had grown into an attractive woman. While he'd always admired her full cheeks, slightly crooked nose, and easy smile, there was now a confidence about her that was compelling.

And even more mesmerizing were her eyes. An unusual combination of gray and green, they were also wide-set and so filled with innocence.

Whenever she gazed at him directly, he could hardly look away.

She'd always reminded him of one of those orphans he'd read about in *Oliver Twist*. Wanting to trust other people, but still staring at the world with a healthy dose of trepidation.

As he continued on by her side, John Michael mentally rolled his eyes. Here he was, waxing poetic about her. Comparing her to an orphan in a Dickens novel.

Hmm. Maybe he was like one of those characters, too. Maybe he was the Artful Dodger, speaking out of both ends of his mouth and wanting too much.

And that, he realized, was the crux of it all. He was still infatuated with Grace. He still ached to know her better. Still ached to be close to her. Wanted to be special to her.

The realization shamed him.

When he'd first met Beth, he was dazzled by her beauty, and then captivated by her outgoing, gregarious family. Those strong descriptors weren't used by accident. He'd felt as if everything about their family could be described in superlatives.

They'd welcomed him into their family with open arms, not caring that he was a Kentucky transplant. They'd embraced his cautious ways, never seeming to notice that he sometimes didn't know how to act around them, thanks to his parents' far quieter manners.

Instead, they seemed to accept him how he was—and then they had taken the time to introduce him to everyone, which made him and his parents feel like they all belonged in Hart County.

But as he got to know Beth, he felt an emptiness in their

relationship. He blamed it on their youth. Then her need to manage him.

Then himself and his stupidity.

As the weeks passed, he'd begun going to their house not to just see Beth but also her sister. Grace. He'd rarely felt so guilty or out of control with his body. It was as if his heart refused to listen to his brain.

"Do you like being a firefighter, John Michael?" Grace asked, interrupting the silence that had fallen between them.

"I do. It's challenging and always busy. I never know what each day will bring."

She looked up at him, intrigued. "I guess it keeps you on your toes."

"It does at that." Thinking about some of the calls he'd gone on, he added, "I've learned so much. Each time we get called out, I feel like I'm pushing myself both physically and mentally. I make a difference, too, which is gratifying. Then, of course, I value the friendships I've made with the other men at the station. In some ways, I feel like the people I work with are my second family."

Still hugging Snooze close to her chest, she glanced up at him again. "What do you do when you aren't fighting fires?"

"I'm on call for twenty-four hours at a time. When I'm at the firehouse I train, help clean the station, and assist everyone with inventory for both the trucks and the ambulance. And sleep and eat," he added with a wink. "I even had to learn to cook for us."

Her eyes widened. "Truly?"

"Yep. All of us are on a rotation. I cook every fourth night when my team is together. I have to tell you, some of my first attempts were awful. I've gotten better, though. Now I make a pretty good plate of spaghetti."

She shook her head. "I never thought about firemen cooking."

"When I first started, I was surprised by how much we do during our shifts."

"You work with Englishers, don't you?"

"There are a couple of Amish men who volunteer if they're

needed. Oh, and we recently hired on an Amish man to be an EMT. It's Noah Freeman. Do you know him?"

She smiled. "*Jah.* I know Noah."

There was a warmth in her voice that he hadn't heard directed toward him. Though he had no business feeling that way, it made him jealous. "He recently married."

"I know. We went to his wedding. I'm surprised you weren't there."

"I was on call." He'd asked to be, so he wouldn't have to cross paths with Beth or Grace.

"That's too bad. It was a lovely day—and a mighty big wedding. Three hundred people!"

"I hated to miss it," he lied.

She paused, pointing to her right. "This way?"

"Uh-huh. It's not much farther. You should see the Lees' house after we climb up this next hill."

She shifted Snooze in her arms.

Belatedly, he realized that he should've been carrying the dog. Snooze wasn't big as far as dogs went, but even carrying a dog his size through the snow could become tiring. "How about you let me take a turn carrying the *hund*?"

"*Nee,*" she said sharply, before catching herself. "I'm sorry. Thank you, but no. I've got him."

"I bet you don't want to let him out of your sight."

"I don't. But that isn't the only reason." Looking pleased, she added, "This is the first time Snooze has let me hold him without tensing up. We're making progress."

"I'm sure he likes being in your arms."

She looked at him sharply. Seemed to consider saying something, but then shut her mouth.

He didn't blame her for being flustered. His comment had been inappropriate.

It really was time to try to smooth things over. They couldn't continue on this way. He couldn't. "I guess we should talk about the elephant in the room, Grace."

"What room is that?"

He wasn't sure if she was teasing him or not. "That's an expression. I guess it's an English one. It, uh, means that we should probably stop avoiding the topic that is on both our minds."

"And what might that be?"

"Beth."

She inhaled sharply. "John Michael, I don't think that's a *gut* idea."

He didn't either, but he also knew that they had no choice. "How is she?"

"Well enough."

"What does that mean?"

"It means that she's doing just fine, in spite of the fact that you broke her heart."

"I'm not going to deny that I could have ended things better, but that was three years ago. Surely, she's moved on?"

Her voice turned hesitant, as if she was trying her best to say what was expected of her instead of what was from her heart. "She's moved on, John. As you said, your relationship ended a long time ago."

"If that's really the case, then why have you been acting so flustered and uneasy around me? Did I do something to you that I wasn't aware of?"

"Of course not. It's just that—" She stopped herself. "Never mind."

"Never mind? I think not. We should clear the air. Talk about everything." Though it would be as painful as getting his teeth pulled, he added, "I could even tell you my side of the story."

Eyes wide, she stared at him for a second before averting her eyes. "I don't believe that's necessary."

"Grace . . ."

"It's freezing out here and you have no coat on."

"I told you I was fine. Besides, it's stopped snowing."

"We need to look out for my cloak."

"I've been looking. If we don't find it today, I'll come out and look tomorrow. Now, tell me Grace, has Beth found someone else?"

She sighed. "*Jah*. I think so."

Grace sounded so vague. Was she evasive on purpose or because she really didn't know? "I hope she has. I'd like her to be happy."

"You really mean that, don't you, John Michael?"

"Of course." As much as Beth had proclaimed at the time to be heartbroken, she'd accepted his decision rather quickly. Though Beth hadn't ever said the words, he'd always gotten the feeling that she, too, had been wishing that there was something more between them. "You might never believe me, but I felt she and I were never meant to be together. Something was missing. I tried to make things better, but I couldn't add something to our relationship that simply wasn't there."

She stopped and stared at him like he had told her something she'd never thought about before. "What was missing?"

How did one describe something that he couldn't explain clearly even to himself? "Something intangible." He pressed a hand to the center of his chest. "A feeling that she was the right woman for me and I was the right man for her."

Grace seemed to dwell on that for a long moment before speaking again. "Beth was practically planning her wedding."

He'd known that—and it had grated on him, too. "That wasn't my fault. I never proposed to her."

"She seemed to think it was understood, though. You came over every Sunday for months. As far as we knew, you didn't visit any other women."

"I didn't. Of course I didn't."

"You befriended all of us. My parents considered you to be one of their own. We all grew attached to you."

"I loved being around your family." That wasn't a lie . . . but, unfortunately, it also wasn't the complete truth. He'd also begun to notice one specific member of the family too much. "Grace, marriage is a bond between two people. It's stronger than families getting along. Even if it wasn't right, I always felt that Beth and I wouldn't be a good match at the end of each day."

She slowed, finally looking like she believed him. "I guess I never thought about relationships that way," she said slowly. "Maybe—Oh! There's my cloak!"

She darted through the field, Snooze lifting his head and looking back at him in alarm as she ran.

"Yeah. I know the feeling, buddy," he muttered, even though he knew the dog couldn't hear him.

His insides felt tangled and twisted, almost as if he had been plunged back into a crevice he'd already climbed out of.

All because he'd come face-to-face with Grace King again. Pretty, quiet, awkward Grace. The girl he'd tried not to notice but had always seen.

The person his heart had told him would give him everything he'd been missing . . . who was also off limits.

Because of that, he'd concentrated on his job and tried to ignore his feelings for her. Actually, he'd hoped that the passing time would change the way he felt about Grace.

It hadn't.

Now here he was again, drawn to the one woman he shouldn't want . . . but still unable to do anything about it.

# CHAPTER 4

John Michael Miller had been kind and attentive and he'd saved Snooze—and her. He'd lent her his coat and was guiding her safely home. He was being helpful in many ways, and she was grateful for it.

But he was not very good at listening to her.

"There's really no need for you to walk me the rest of the way, John. I'll be fine." Grace knew she was being more than a little ungracious. But the Lees' house was looming up ahead and Snooze was getting heavy in her arms.

And John Michael's companionship? Well, it was something she didn't need to subject herself to for long periods of time. Every time she let her mind ease, she found herself rethinking his and Beth's breakup from a new perspective.

Found herself wondering if maybe her family had gotten it wrong.

That there really were more important things to worry about besides weekly visits and plans.

Maybe what really counted in a relationship were evenings spent in private, when it was just the two of them. When there was no more business to the day, only hours to fill before sleep.

What if there wasn't *anything* there—no contentment or sense of peace, no sparks of desire?

That would be difficult, indeed.

"Let me see you safely back."

"I'll be fine."

"Please, Grace. Allow me to help you."

With anyone else, she would've found his words and his offer to be chivalrous. Grace knew she needed to keep that in mind. They walked the rest of the way in silence. As they got closer, his brow furrowed.

"Grace, I know you aren't a little girl, but I can't help but worry about you and this job of yours. Do you ever get afraid to live in all these strange houses by yourself?"

"Not at all." Yes, her voice had a new edge to it, but she couldn't help herself. She'd been doing this job for quite some time now. It wasn't his place to be questioning it.

"Are you sure? That is a mighty big home. Some might even call it a mansion. You don't find being by yourself in this big place off-putting?"

The house had six bedrooms, seven bathrooms, three fire-places, a library, a dining room, and a breakfast room with some-thing called a butler's pantry next to it. It had living areas on all three floors. It was the biggest house she'd ever stayed in, that was true. But until that moment, she hadn't found it off-putting at all. Merely, really big—and never something she would want to clean. Now, though, she felt a shudder pass through her at the thought of living there by herself for another thirteen days. "Don't worry about me. I'm used to this."

"I understand." Gazing at the stone structure again, he said, "Where do you sleep?"

"Upstairs. Why?"

"If someone broke in the front or back doors, you might not hear it if you were upstairs asleep."

That was true . . . but why would he say such a thing? "I'll be fine," she said again.

As they neared the front door, he grinned. "All right. I'll leave you alone. I'm just glad we found Snooze."

"Me, too. I wouldn't have, if not for you."

He pointed to the footprints that headed around the side of the house. "Looks like you had quite the time of it, searching around the yard for him."

She nodded . . . just as she realized that those were not her foot-prints. Hers no doubt had been covered up by the falling snow. These? These were fresher and from bigger feet. Staring at the large prints that disappeared off to the side, she wondered who had been there . . . and why they had been walking around the house's perimeter.

John Michael touched her arm.

She practically jumped a foot into the air.

"Sorry!" He shook his head. "It seems I have a lot to make up for, don't I? Obviously, you are still upset about what happened between me and Beth. And now I'm bringing up all kinds of issues with you living alone."

She was used to staying in other people's homes all the time. She'd never felt scared. Maybe it was because she always had the owners' dogs or cats with her, and they were excellent at watching out for their property. Then, too, they were in the middle of cave country in Kentucky, not in a big city like Nashville or Louisville.

But those footprints . . . they were definitely unsettling. Immediately, she began thinking of all sorts of awful scenarios. Maybe someone had broken into the Lees' home. Maybe someone was still outside, watching them.

But if she mentioned any of that to him, John Michael would grow even more concerned. Maybe he'd even try to convince her to call the sheriff or leave.

She didn't want to do either of those things, especially since she wanted him to see her as a responsible woman, not a scared and needy child.

Therefore, against her better judgment, she lied. *"Jah.* At first I was so sure that Snooze with his little legs couldn't go very far. I kept walking around the house and calling his name."

"You didn't notice his tracks running toward the woods?"

Of course she had. "Obviously not." Hating that she sounded so, well, stupid, she stepped closer to the front door. "I've learned my lesson now, though! Snooze won't be going outside without a leash ever again."

"I hope not. You should keep it by the door so you don't forget it when you leave."

"That's a *gut* idea." Of course she was mentally rolling her eyes. Did he not think she did anything right?

Placing her hand on the door, she murmured, "It's all over now, though. I better get on inside."

"All right." He paused. "Are we ever going to be okay, Grace?"

His sincerity punched holes in the many excuses she had had for not forgiving him. It made her feel slightly embarrassed, too. After all, though she loved her sister, she wasn't unaware that Beth had as many flaws as she herself did. As everyone did.

And, well, love had to exist between two people. Who was she to judge if John Michael hadn't felt that he and Beth should be together forever?

"We are better," she said at last.

"Promise?"

"I promise." She spoke from the heart, too. She wanted the two of them to be better.

"I'll take that. Well, I guess I should go . . . unless you'd like me to walk inside with you and make sure everything is okay?"

That sense of foreboding she'd been feeling had grown even stronger. For a moment, she considered taking him up on it.

But to what end?

"Thank you for the offer, but that's not necessary."

"All right, then. Good-bye, Grace. I hope you and Snooze have a good evening." He smiled. Another one of those heart-stopping, gorgeous smiles that she used to dream about years ago.

He turned and walked away before she could summon the nerve to reply.

She tried to tell herself that the hint of disappointment and loss she was feeling wasn't real . . . just as she was attempting to pretend that the fresh footsteps in the snow were nothing to be alarmed about.

# CHAPTER 5

As soon as Grace released Snooze, he darted into the living room. She stood in the open foyer and listened for any sign that she wasn't alone.

She didn't hear a thing.

Summoning her courage, she strode to the kitchen, picked up the Lees' phone, and carried it with her as she walked through the house. She checked the locks on the windows. Made sure the doors in the back of the house were still shut tight.

When she was satisfied that she was safe and secure, she pushed her fears to one side and concentrated on her job instead. She gave Snooze a bath and dried him carefully with two towels. Then she fed him supper and did a load of laundry.

After she'd taken her own shower and had her own supper, she turned on the Lees' television. Though she didn't usually ever turn it on, she'd been desperate to find something to take her mind off her worries . . . and her reunion with John Michael. But even though *Rudolph the Red-Nosed Reindeer* was rather entertaining, his adventures didn't help ease her mind.

Eating three scones hadn't helped, either.

As the hour grew late, she began reading, hoping to become so engrossed in the pages of the book that she'd forget her own problems. It took a while, and it finally helped. She drifted off to sleep thinking not of her problems but of the heroine in the book she was reading and her trials in the Alaskan wilderness.

Then, like unwelcome houseguests, her thoughts were invaded again—she was dreaming . . . she was back at home, in her own bed.

Her bedroom window opened with a clatter. The movement knocked over a candle. Next thing she knew, her quilt was on fire. Afraid and alone, she started screaming and ran for the door, but it was locked. Just as she started banging on it, calling for her parents to help her, John Michael appeared at her window, beckoning her to him. Just as she reached for his hand, her sister opened her door and called her away.

As the fire tore through her bedding, she froze in her tracks, wanting to take John's hand to safety but afraid to ignore her sister's pleas. She was so distraught, she cried out, trying to catch her breath—

And realized the fire existed only in her dream.

She'd found it almost impossible to fall asleep after that. She tossed and turned, reliving all her conversations with John Michael and flinching every time the house creaked or groaned. She remained curled up in a ball and thoroughly miserable until she fell back to sleep again.

GRACE WOKE UP late, feeling achy and sore—and far too jumpy. She wondered if she was going to be dwelling on John Michael's warnings for the next two weeks. When she found herself jumping when a branch fell in the distance, Grace feared it was likely.

Determined to try to find some ray of light in the last twenty-four hours, she focused on her new and improved relationship with Snooze.

The dog, however, seemed to have an extremely short memory, for his cuddles were once again a thing of the past.

He wasn't grateful that she'd rescued him out of the snow and the dirty pile of straw. He hadn't appreciated being carried the whole way home, snug and warm next to her body while she lugged him around, all fourteen pounds of him.

Nope, he was back to giving her the cold shoulder again. Actually, he seemed to be nursing a Great Dane–sized grudge against her. He wouldn't touch his breakfast until she left the room. It seemed he even liked to dine in private.

Unfortunately for Snooze, Grace's whole body was tired, her left foot was slightly swollen from her stumble, and she was emotionally drained.

"You're just gonna have to get used to me," she said as she stretched out on the couch by his side. "This is the coziest couch, and both the fireplace and the Christmas tree are in this room. I'm not going to allow you to have the entire room to yourself."

Snooze, after giving her a rather disdainful glare, snorted. Then he flipped over on his side so that his back was to her.

She sighed and picked up her stationery to write her parents a letter. Her pen hovered over the paper as she tried to think of what to write that wouldn't sound too sad or lonely. For a moment, she considered sharing how she'd literally run into John Michael, but knew that wouldn't bring forth any joy.

The knock at the door was almost a welcome relief. When it was followed by the merry chime of the doorbell, Snooze burst out of his quilt like he was offended.

Before she could get to her feet, he was at the door, barking and running in circles.

"Hush, Snooze," she soothed. "I bet it's just the UPS man." He'd come almost every day with a new package. She peeked out the window, prepared to see a man in a brown uniform retreating back . . . but caught John Michael staring back at her instead.

With a feeling of foreboding, she scooped Snooze up in her arms and then opened the door. "John Michael," she greeted hesitantly. "Is everything all right?"

"You know what? I'm not sure."

"Beg your pardon?"

"Let's talk about this inside." He took a step closer, then paused. "Please, Grace?"

"Well, all right." She gestured for him to enter as best she could, considering that Snooze was both squirming and barking once again.

John Michael only laughed. After closing the door behind him, he knelt down to where she'd just deposited the dog. "Hey, buddy," he murmured gently, scratching him just behind his ears. "How are you feeling after your adventure?"

Snooze, the traitor that he was, wagged his tail and stepped closer to their visitor. He even went as far as to tilt his head up so John Michael could scratch under his chin.

Grace shook her head in dismay. "He never allows me to do that."

"No? That's surprising."

"It's frustrating, that's what it is."

"He'll come around, I bet." John Michael's lips twitched.

"One can only hope."

When he stood up to face her, all traces of amusement were gone from his face. "Grace, we need to talk."

"About what?" She really hoped it wasn't going to be about Beth.

"I couldn't sleep last night, Grace. I kept thinking about yesterday's adventure."

Glad that he didn't want to rehash the past again, she smiled. "I did the same thing. If not for you, I might have lost Snooze forever."

Instead of looking pleased that they were talking about his heroism, John Michael shrugged off her praise. "I wasn't thinking about Snooze, Grace."

"Oh?" Just like that, her apprehension returned.

"*Jah*. You see, I was thinking about those footprints. This morning when I was bringing in a stack of wood for the fireplace, I noticed my own tracks in the snow. And that's when I realized something. Those footprints next to this house weren't yours. Yours would have been covered up by the snow that had fallen while you were gone."

She could either lie or she could tell the truth. "I know that."

He blinked slowly, like he was trying to understand her fib. "If you knew, why didn't you correct me?"

"I didn't know what purpose it would serve," she said honestly. "I didn't want to worry you, and I didn't want to start jumping to conclusions and start looking for problems where there weren't any."

"But someone could have been here. You could have gotten attacked."

"But I wasn't."

Impatience entered his tone. "Don't be pert, Grace. I've been worried."

"I appreciate your concern. All I'm trying to say and point out is that despite your worries, I am fine."

He stuffed his hands in his coat pockets. "So, what did you do when you got inside? Did you call the sheriff and ask him to stop by?"

"*Nee.*"

His voice turned even more strained. "Grace, did you do anything last night?"

She nodded. "I walked around the house and checked all the doors and windows. When everything seemed secure, I went about my business and gave Snooze a bath."

A muscle in his jaw twitched. "That's it? You could have been in danger last night. You still could be."

"I was fine last night." Except for her scary dream. "John Michael, to be honest, I was a little worried last night, but I also know the danger of jumping to conclusions and fearing the worst." She waved a hand. "Those footsteps could have belonged to one of the Lees' workers. Mrs. Lee told me that she might have people stop by from time to time to check on the gardens and fixtures they have in the back."

"*Jah.* I'm sure they do a lot of work outside during snowstorms."

"I locked the doors, and I'm careful, too. I'm not going to take chances with Snooze."

Staring at her intently, he lowered his voice. "I'm worried about you, Grace. Not the dog."

"I appreciate that. Now, would you like to come the rest of the way inside and have a cup of tea or coffee?"

His dark eyes softened. "I wish I could, but I need to head over to the firehouse."

She noticed then that his wool coat wasn't buttoned and he was wearing his fireman's uniform underneath. He had on navy blue pants, boots, and a long-sleeved light-blue shirt that had buttons at the collar. The words *Hart County Fire Department* were embroidered in red on the breast pocket of his coat.

"The chief is holding a couple of meetings today. I'm not supposed to be on, but I should only be there for a couple of hours." He shifted and pulled out a card from his pocket. "Before I go, I want to give you this." He pointed to the printed information. "See, there's the firehouse's phone number."

"I do know how to call 911, John Michael."

"Of course you do. But you can use this number in case you need something that's not an emergency. Like if you're just worried or something. Or, um, want to talk."

She swallowed. What would her sister say? "I don't know . . ."

He curved his hands around her palm and pressed the card there. "Please take it. Knowing that you have a way to easily get ahold of me will ease my mind."

She felt her cheeks heat, but whether it was from the touch of his hands or the way he was gazing at her, she didn't know. "*Danke.* I will put it by the Lees' telephone."

"*Gut.*" He exhaled. "All right. I'll be there for a few hours, then I'm going home and helping my *daed.* Tomorrow I'm on from seven until the following morning."

"All right."

"So call if you need me."

"I will."

"In two days, I'll stop by again. Will that be all right?"

Before she gave herself time to think about the wisdom of that, she nodded. "If you want to."

"I want to." He smiled then. "Now lock the door," he ordered. "And call me or the police if you see more tracks."

"Yes, John Michael. I promise."

His eyes warmed before he walked out. After she watched him leave, she did lock the door. And then did set the card right next to the Lees' phone.

Just in case.

# CHAPTER 6

The alarm bells started ringing barely two hours after John Michael had fallen asleep in his bunk room at the firehouse. Thanks to hours of practice and his years of experience, his body sprang into action almost before his mind could catch up.

Within seconds, he was out of bed and shoving his feet into the boots he'd learned to leave neatly by the door. The bright lights and activity of the garage bay shook off the last of John's grogginess. He ran past the dayroom and hustled down the steps just seconds after Captain Butler himself.

The captain was speaking into his radio in between barking orders to the engineer. "Ladder and pumper trucks!" he called out as he stepped into his turnout gear.

As the bells continued and Hank, the crew's engineer, fired up the ladder truck, John Michael pulled on his own gear, grabbed his helmet and work gloves, then ran to his usual place in the ladder truck—the jump seat in the back of the vehicle.

"We've got ourselves a house fire over in Horse Cave, y'all!" Captain Butler called out from the passenger seat as Hank turned on the lights and sirens and sped down the driveway. "Word is the building's abandoned, but we'll need to check. You copy?"

"Copy," John Michael called out, grabbing the door handle as Hank took a sharp right turn. Sean and Anderson were following behind them in the pumper truck. Its lights flashed against the snow and cast red and blue beams across the empty streets.

John Michael felt that same burst of adrenaline that he did

during every call. He loved his job. Loved that they helped people—and loved the excitement of it. There was something curiously fulfilling about knowing that he was capable of fighting a fire.

There was also something gratifying in knowing that he was also part of a team. An accepted and appreciated part of a team. Sean, Anderson, and Hank were English and far more experienced firefighters. Captain Zack Butler had twelve years and started out in Frankfort.

The other men talked about college basketball while they went through their check-offs; John Michael focused on his own routine. He still got a little nervous every time they went out, and because of that he stayed silent and preferred to concentrate on the work they were about to do. He liked checking and double-checking his equipment.

And though he'd never made a fuss about it, he also said a quiet prayer to himself. *Lord, give me your strength and your protection during today's fight. Place your healing hands on our victims and ask your angels to look over the other members of our team.*

When he opened his eyes, the truck was making another hard right. He held on tight as the vehicle straightened and then headed down Highway 88.

"We first in?" Hank asked.

"Yep," the captain said. "Looks like we're five minutes away. You hear me, Miller?"

"Yes, Captain."

John Michael could hear other sirens in the distance. He knew that an ambulance and very likely the sheriff or deputy would be en route, too.

"I've been on the radio with the sheriff. Witnesses said that no one lives there, that it's been abandoned. But still, we've gotta check," the captain continued.

There was no time to respond as the truck squealed to a stop and they all bolted out.

It was a small house, really no more than a shack. And it was consumed by flames. Only the thick blanket of snow on the ground had saved what looked like a field of dried grass and brush.

What followed was what he'd always described as an intricate dance, reinforced by hours of practice and instruction. Captain Butler met the pumper truck. Hank, his breathing apparatus already engaged, led John Michael to the house. John Michael held the jump line, bracing himself for when the hose was fully charged.

John Michael could faintly hear the captain continuing to communicate with the other truck and the chief, checking in with reports and simultaneously shouting orders and information into his earpiece.

The heat from the fire was intense, making John Michael more grateful than ever for his gear. It was heavy—near seventy pounds—but worth every ounce.

Dragging the hose closer, John Michael braced himself for the first surge of water to spray. He concentrated on fighting the flames and following Hank's hand and arm signals. As each minute passed and the flames were steadily extinguished, he felt the familiar sensations of both energy and satisfaction. He was helping his community. Helping his neighbors. Working with others for a greater cause.

Those were the things his grandparents and parents had drilled into him at a young age, and though he hadn't ever considered being a firefighter until he began searching for new meaning in his life, after breaking things off with Beth, John Michael now realized that he was meant to be a firefighter. He worked well under pressure. He was a good team player.

And he was also far braver than he'd ever imagined he could be. But surely that was the Lord's doing.

When Hank signaled for the hoses to stop, John still held his at the ready—until he felt satisfied that all flames were extinguished. Only then did he relax his stance.

With a sigh of relief, he pushed up his face mask and took deep breaths of the frigid air. It felt soothing. Like a balm in the midst of the chaos.

"You good, John?" Hank called out.

"I am. You?"

Hank grinned at him, traces of soot and ash on his face. "Good as ever. I love this job."

"Me, too." John Michael couldn't help but grin back.

"You pray for us?"

"I did."

"Good." Hank reached out and thumped him on the back. "I knew you were the right addition to us. Knew it."

"You always say that."

"Because it's true."

John grinned at the words. The first time he admitted to praying for all of them, he'd felt a little wary. Not because he was embarrassed about his practice, but because he didn't want the men to act as if he wasn't completely focused on the job at hand.

But to his surprise, none of the men had ever acted as if his prayers were anything but a blessing to the unit. Some of the men, like Captain Butler, never mentioned it. But Hank always did. It was like the man felt he needed all of John Michael's prayers to see him through each call out.

Hank slapped him on the back again before joining Anderson and the captain. It was John Michael's job to put the hoses away and make sure that no one had inadvertently left out any supplies in the area. After carefully stowing his helmet and gloves, he opened up the toggles on his uniform to allow his body to cool, then began work on rolling the hoses.

He knew rookies on other crews hated this part of the job. John Michael had never minded it, though. He liked order in his life. Carefully setting the truck's equipment to rights gave him a lot of satisfaction.

Then, too, were the stories his trainers and instructors had told him about instances where firefighters' lives were in danger because someone hadn't taken the time to check and double-check everything.

Just as John finished, he became aware that the other men weren't slowly coming back his way or joking with Deputy Beck or Mitch Quinn, the ambulance driver who had pulled up behind the truck.

Instead, all the men were circled around Anderson and Captain Butler, who were standing in the rubble. Curious, John Michael headed toward them.

Hank looked up and, after saying something to Mitch, walked closer. "Looks like I spoke too soon," he said to John.

"What do you mean?"

"This fire wasn't an accident. We found a metal trash can and the remains of lighter fluid. It was set on purpose."

From time to time, they came across fires that were set on purpose. Teenagers are notorious for starting fires in dumpsters, just to see what would happen.

This was nothing new. Usually, it was discovered that a fire was started in a cardboard box or with a piece of wood. "I'm curious as to why someone would use a metal trash can," John wondered.

"They didn't care about it being found. All they cared about was that it was bad enough to keep all of us and the sheriff department busy."

"If that was the case, I'd say they got what they wanted," John murmured. The building had been engulfed in flames when they pulled up. "But why would they want to do that?" It seemed like a waste of time to him.

Hank grunted as he stepped closer. "I'm almost afraid to find out."

# CHAPTER 7

"Did you hear about the fire, Grace?" Irene Keim asked as she approached Grace's booth at Bill's Diner.

Grace nodded as Irene poured her a cup of coffee. "It's terrible. Such a tragedy, too." John Michael's mother had stopped by the Lees' house yesterday afternoon. She brought Grace a container of bean soup and a plate of snowball cookies, mentioning that her son had asked her to check on her since he had been at work.

Grace had at first felt awkward and embarrassed. John Michael had gone out of his way to help—both with Snooze and again when he came over to check on her. But instead of practicing forgiveness and concentrating on the present, she treated John Michael almost like an enemy.

Then Mrs. Miller told her the news about the fire. Grace was frightened for John . . . and then was shocked to hear that there was a rumor about the fire being set on purpose. It seemed particularly foolish and scary. Grace couldn't imagine why someone would do such a thing.

"I feel so sorry for the people affected, Irene. Have you heard who it was?"

She set the carafe of coffee on the table and shook her head. "*Nee*. I even asked Lora, who you know is married to Deputy Beck. But she didn't hear anything, either."

"It is an awful thing to happen at any time, but it seems even more awful at Christmas."

Irene nodded. "I've been thinking the same thing." Smiling

wearily, she said, "But if I've learned anything lately, it's that God doesn't choose only some people and some places to pass out burdens. He's an equal opportunity giver!"

Grace smiled at the quip, though she knew Irene was speaking from her own personal pain as much as the latest tragedy in Hart County. "I'm starting to learn that while He does give out burdens, they never seem to be more than we can handle."

"I would have to agree," said Irene, "though I would be lying if I didn't say that sometimes I wish my burdens were a little lighter." As she lifted up her pad of paper, she continued. "Now, let's talk about something far better. Do you know what you'd like for breakfast?"

"I do. I'll have scrambled eggs, sausage, and grits."

"You got it."

Scanning the brightly colored menu again, Grace said, "Oh! I'd like some pancakes, too."

"Blueberry or buttermilk?"

"Blueberry," she said, already imagining how good the pancakes would taste. Since she was eating by herself, her meals had become sketchy at best, usually only a can of soup or a sandwich. Hopefully, this big breakfast would sustain her until close to suppertime.

Irene smiled. "Anything else, Grace?"

"Orange juice?"

"I'll get that now," she replied with a chuckle.

Grace sipped her coffee and watched the bustle around the diner. Over the last year, it seemed to have gotten busier. There had even been some instances on a Friday or Saturday when she and her family had to wait for a table.

When the door opened again, she lifted her head expectantly, hoping someone might come in that she recognized and could chat with. She really was missing her sisters and Jennifer!

But when she saw it was John Michael walking in with Noah Freeman, she felt her skin heat. Honestly, what were the odds? After going years without seeing him at all, or only from a distance, now they seemed to be almost regularly running into each other!

Staring at him a bit longer than necessary, she looked away.

But it was too late. John Michael had noticed her, too. After murmuring something to Noah, he walked through the crowded dining room and stopped by her side. "Grace, it's *gut* to see you. Boy, twice in less than a week, too."

Feeling like half the restaurant was watching their exchange, she felt a little self-conscious but determined to finally put the past behind her. "I was just thinking the same thing."

"I hope you are doing well. Is your ankle all right?"

"My ankle?" Realizing he was speaking of her clumsy stumble in the field, she waved a hand. "Oh, it's a little bruised but otherwise none too worse for wear. How are you?"

"I'm *gut,* too." Just as he looked like he was about to turn around and join Noah, she caught a bandage on the top of his hand.

"Are you hurt? Did you injure yourself in the fire?"

"This?" He looked at his hand like he'd forgotten a bandage was attached to his skin. "It ain't anything, just a cut."

It seemed like a pretty big bandage for a small cut. "Are you sure that's all it is?"

"*Jah.* I'm fine. I wouldn't be a firefighter if I didn't sport a couple of cuts every now and then."

"It's such a dangerous job."

"It is," he said slowly, like he was attempting to navigate his way through an increasingly surprising conversation. "But I can handle it. I appreciate your concern, though."

She heard the caution in his voice, and she didn't blame him for not being sure how to handle this new, kinder version of herself. Forging ahead, she said, "I know I have no right to feel this way, but now that we've reconnected, I think I'm going to worry about you every time I hear there is a fire in the area."

"There's no need for you to worry. I take every precaution and my captain makes sure we're well trained."

"Though my brain might agree, I have a feeling I'll still worry."

Tenderness appeared in his eyes before he blinked it away. "I can understand that. I mean, I would worry about you if the situations were reversed."

She couldn't help but smile at that scenario. "I'm fairly sure that the only fires I'll ever be fighting are the ones in the fireplace."

"It will be a blessing if that's your only experience fighting flames."

His expression was so earnest. Truly, the things he said! "I'm kind of a scaredy-cat, so I hope that's the case," Grace admitted. "But I will keep you in my prayers, if you don't mind."

"I don't mind at all, especially if you keep my whole crew in them. Firefighters can't have enough prayers sent to heaven."

What a conversation they were having! It felt like they were talking about two different things at the same time. His safety and their relationship.

Both tangents seemed very personal.

Seeking to lighten the tone, she smiled. "Consider it done."

His light-brown eyes skimmed over her. "How did you get all the way over here? You didn't drive a buggy all this way, did ya?"

"*Nee.* I hired a driver to take me back and forth." A buggy would have made the journey take at least an hour. It would have been a bitter-cold trip, too.

"I'm glad. The roads are slick."

"The driver drives a Jeep, so I was safe."

"You just come in for breakfast?"

"*Nee.* I'm going to do some shopping, too. It's nice spending part of my Saturday among people instead of only Snooze."

"I imagine so."

When they exchanged smiles, Grace felt something new pass between them. Maybe it was the beginnings of a friendship? She wasn't sure.

Looking disappointed to be leaving her side, he gestured toward a booth. "I need to join my friend, but I wanted to tell ya that *mei mamm* said she had a nice visit with you. Thank you for treating her so graciously."

The compliment stung, but given the way she'd treated him during their search and rescue of Snooze, she supposed she couldn't blame him. "No need to thank me. I enjoyed visiting with your mother. It was nice of her to stop by. The days can be long."

He rocked back on his heels. "I still intend to stop by again one day soon."

She smiled. "Then maybe I'll see you."

After knocking his knuckles on the table, he walked to the booth he was sharing with Noah. Unable to stop herself, she watched his retreating back.

She was so glad she'd let go of that anger she'd been feeling toward him. They were on their way to becoming friends. Though she had a feeling she was going to be having to explain their renewed friendship to her family when they returned, she felt good about her decision. Moving forward really had been the right thing to do.

Just as Grace was about to turn away, she caught sight of an older Amish woman sitting alone. Something about her pulled on her heartstrings, though Grace wasn't sure exactly why. After all, she was sitting by herself as well.

But maybe it was because the woman looked a little dejected?

Unable to stop herself, Grace continued to study the woman. She looked so very alone. Rather unkempt and exhausted, too.

When the woman turned her head to watch a family with four children rush in through the door, Grace studied her more intently. Thanks to her pet-sitting job, she knew a lot of people in the community.

But this woman? Other than a feeling like she should know her, she couldn't place her.

When the woman turned her head and looked directly back at her, Grace averted her head, feeling self-conscious. No doubt the woman didn't appreciate being stared at.

She pulled her latest library book out of her tote bag and carefully opened it to where she'd left off last. It was a mystery set in Shipshewana, Indiana, filled with Amish folks, a little humor, and two murders. She dove into the story, glad to have something else to concentrate on.

"HERE YOU GO, Grace," Irene said with a chuckle as she placed not one but three plates on the table. "Eggs, sausage, grits, pancakes, and Bill even threw in a buttermilk biscuit fresh from the oven! A monster breakfast for probably the littlest person in the restaurant."

Pushing aside her book, Grace chuckled, too. Her slim build and constant appetite had always been both a mystery and a sore spot with her sisters. They'd often said it simply wasn't fair that she could eat so much without gaining weight.

She used to be self-conscious about it. But now?—she was thankful to have one less thing to worry about. "*Danke*. It looks *wonderbaar.*"

"I hope you will enjoy it. Bill said he'd give you a piece of pie to take home if you clean your plate."

Grace giggled. "Uh-oh. I fear I'm so hungry that I just might do that. I'd love to take a piece of Bill's pie back with me."

"Why are you so hungry? Is your *mamm* not feeding you?"

It was a joke in the county that Josephine King could bake circles around most anyone. "My mother is probably cooking up a storm for *the rest* of my family. They ain't here. They went to my grandparents for Christmas. I had to stay behind for a job."

"Are you watching another lucky pet?"

"I am. I'm pet sitting at the Lees'."

Irene's eyes widened. "You're staying in that big house by yourself? For how long?"

"For two weeks."

Irene frowned. "Sounds like a long time, especially at Christmas."

It was, but she sure wasn't going to make Irene worry about it. "They have an adorable dachshund named Snooze. He's keeping me great company," she lied. Patting the book, she said, "I also have a stack of mysteries to read. I'll be fine."

Irene looked at the book doubtfully before focusing back on

Grace. "I'll bring you that piece of pie in a container in a few minutes. What kind would you like? Pumpkin, pecan, or apple?"

"Pecan, please."

"You got it. Enjoy your breakfast."

After bowing her head and giving thanks, Grace opened back up the book and dug into her meal, savoring every bite of food that she hadn't had to make. When she was about halfway done, Irene came back. "Here's your pie and your check for when you're ready."

"Hey, Irene? Who is that lady sitting over there by herself?"

Irene turned to look. When she faced Grace again, there was a look of bitterness on her pretty face. "That's Miss Schultz."

"Miss Dorma Schultz?"

"*Jah.* The very one."

"I was just talking to, uh, someone about her the other day. It turns out the Millers' house is on the Schultzes' old farm."

"They were once very wealthy, weren't they?"

Grace raised her eyebrows. "I would imagine she is now, since she sold off all that farmland."

"If her relatives had let her keep any of it, you mean."

"What?"

"She lives on her own in a small house just a couple of blocks from here. Bill says her extended family volunteered to handle her money—and promptly took most of it."

"That's awful! Wasn't there something she could do?"

"Probably, if she was in better health."

"Is she sick? What's wrong with her?"

Irene shook her head. "There's more to the story, but I can't share it now. You've got a meal to finish and I've got customers to wait on."

"Oh! Yes, of course."

When she had just about cleaned her plate, Grace set her fork down and closed the book with a contented sigh. Getting out of the house had been a mighty good idea. The food was wonderful, her book got even more exciting, and she was able to chat with

John Michael without offending him. She even got to chat with Irene and a few other acquaintances.

And Miss Dorma!

Feeling terrible that she hadn't already walked over to say hello, Grace decided to forgo the rest of her errands and go sit with her. Who knows? Maybe Miss Dorma would even like her slice of pecan pie to take home.

Grace paid and hurried to the washroom to clean up. But when she came back out, Miss Dorma had already left.

All that remained was a neatly folded dollar bill next to her coffee cup.

# CHAPTER 8

After they ordered their food and downed their first cups of steaming hot coffee, John Michael noticed that Noah's attention had wandered. Every couple of minutes, Noah would stare at something directly behind him.

"What's going on?" John asked after turning around and seeing nothing out of the ordinary.

Noah blinked. "Huh? Oh, sorry. I can't seem to stop looking at that lady sitting behind you. I think she almost looks like Dorma Schultz, but that can't be right. I keep trying to place her. Has that ever happened to you?"

"More than I'd like to admit." He turned around again but only saw the back of an elderly lady as she was walking out the door. "Was that her?"

"Uh-huh."

Now John Michael was determined to get a better look. He craned his neck to see her turn . . . and then realized that Noah hadn't been wrong. "That was Miss Dorma, all right."

"I know she's gotten older, but she don't look good."

"No, she don't." The woman he saw looked like a shadow of her former self. Whereas she used to be spry and almost athletic-looking, she now looked frail, as if a harsh wind could blow her over. She also had only an old wool shawl wrapped around her shoulders. It couldn't have been enough to guard against the cold.

As John Michael watched her walk down the street, he said, "The first time I glanced behind me, I didn't recognize her at all."

It made him sad, too. He liked her so much when he was a little boy. Though they hadn't been close, he would always take the time to say hello to her if he saw her on the street or in a store.

"When did you see Miss Dorma last?" Noah asked.

Looking at her as she passed from view made John realize just how long it must have been.

"Oh, boy. Not in years." He laughed softly. "I'll tell you how I knew it was actually her—it was that posture! I don't think I've ever met another person who stands as straight as she does. When we were little, my mother used to tell my sisters to stand proud and straight like Miss Dorma. I grew up thinking that Miss Dorma could do no wrong."

Noah grinned. "I thought the same thing! Though, I did used to wonder where she got that scar on her cheek. Me and my siblings always wanted to ask, but we never did."

"I'd forgotten about that! I never asked her, either."

"Of course not! She'd say we were being impertinent."

"And we would have had no idea what that meant and would be afraid to ask," John said, enjoying the trip down memory lane.

"My brother Silas used to shovel her walkway every time it snowed. He always complained that she never paid him even a dime. All she ever did was tell him that he was a good boy."

"He wanted her to pay him?" asked John.

"Maybe, maybe not. All I know is that her treating him like a youngster when he was fifteen grated on his nerves."

John Michael chuckled, thinking he could imagine her saying such things very easily. "Knowing Dorma, she probably said that on purpose because she thought he was getting too big for his britches. She used to be quite a character, ain't so?"

"*Jah*. She cared about everyone, like they were special to her." Noah sipped his coffee and mused, "You know, my parents said they liked to watch her in action after church. She'd herd us *kinner* around like a sheepdog."

"One time she had me washing tables after church before I remembered that I had been hoping to take off with my friends."

"I was right there with you, John. My siblings and I both loved and feared her at the same time." Noah's amused expression faded. "Her skin looked a bit sallow. I wonder if she is sick."

John knew Noah had extensive medical training as an EMT. "I think you may be right. At first I thought she was simply looking frail, but that isn't it."

"She seems vacant," Noah said. "Almost like she is confused. That's why I couldn't seem to take my eyes off of her."

"I should try to figure out where she lives now and check on her."

"That's a good idea, John." Clearing his throat, Noah said, "Have you heard *anything* about her lately?"

"Funny you should ask. Grace King and I were just speaking of Miss Dorma the other day. Grace is pet sitting over at Mr. and Mrs. Lee's house. If you remember, they bought part of the Schultz land and my family bought up the other half."

"That was some time ago."

"At least ten or twelve years past." The lump that had formed in his throat seemed to be growing bigger by the second. "*Mei mamm* and an aunt saw her maybe a year ago. I seem to remember that she was staying with relatives. I'm going to ask the captain about it at the firehouse. Maybe we could stop by, do a wellness check."

"I'll be happy to join you," Noah said.

"*Danke.* I'll let you know what they say."

After Irene brought them more coffee, they continued their conversation. "One of my aunts told me a while back that Miss Dorma was living in a little *haus* on the edge of town," John Michael said. "I remember wondering how she felt about living so close to people after having hundreds of acres all her own."

"You could ask her that when you stop by."

"I will." Feeling even more certain that he owed Dorma a visit, John Michael said, "You know what? I think I owe it to Miss Dorma to stop by as soon as possible, even if the captain doesn't want us to go as a member of the fire department. She did so much for all of us."

"It's settled, then. Next time we're both off work on the same days, we'll find out where she lives and say hello."

Glad that they had made plans, John Michael felt himself relax. "Let's talk about something else. How is your Sadie and the babe?"

Noah smiled. "*Wonderbaar.* The *boppli* is doing well and Sadie has taken to motherhood like she was born to care for babies. Nothing seems to worry her too much or make her anxious."

"I'm glad you're happy."

"Me, too. To be honest, I didn't expect to fall in love anytime soon. I thought I'd concentrate on my job for the next five or six years, then eventually find the right partner. I'm mighty glad I was wrong."

Thinking about Grace, he said, "I suppose one never knows what God has in store for us."

"If I've learned anything from being an EMT, it's that life is rarely neat or organized. The Lord plans things in His own time. It's up to us to simply hold on."

"That's good advice."

"Sorry you two have been waiting forever!" Irene said as she hurried over with a tray in her hands. "Bill wasn't happy with the way your poached eggs turned out, so he made you a new plate, Noah."

"They look fine, indeed. Worth the wait."

"And here is your club sandwich for breakfast, John Michael."

"It looks fantastic. So good I'm going to pretend I didn't hear the way you criticized my meal."

"Sorry, but you do have to admit that it's odd. I've never known of another customer besides you to order sandwiches for breakfast."

Holding a triangle in his hand, John grinned at her. "I surely don't know why. Sandwiches are perfect most any time of the day, especially at breakfast."

She laughed. "I'll take your word for it, John. And, Noah, for once, try and relax for a few minutes. You usually wolf down your sandwich and go."

After she left their side, John Michael grinned at Noah. "You can act like you're so busy you have to eat on the run, but I know better."

"What is that?"

"You are in a hurry to get home to your wife."

Noah grinned again. "I can't deny it. I feel like I waited all my life for Sadie to come into my life. Why would I not want to spend as much time with her when I can?"

As John Michael closed his eyes to give thanks, he realized Noah's words hit close to home. He'd already waited a long time to have a chance with Grace King. It would be foolish for him not to try to spend as much time with her as he could.

After all, who knew when the Lord would give him another such opportunity?

# CHAPTER 9

Three hours later, John Michael found himself helping his father oil and polish their sled, and thinking about Miss Dorma again. He had a job where he risked his life for others, was proud of it, and liked knowing that he was able to give back to the community. Realizing that he'd essentially forgotten about Dorma Schultz was hard to accept. He was ashamed to realize that he'd received so much from her but had not spared her a moment's thought when she wasn't around.

Worse, from the looks of that shawl, she was in need.

After washing off the worst of the dirt and sanding the sled's runners, he and his father turned it right-side up and got to work on the rest of it.

John Michael got busy rubbing some grapeseed oil into the leather of the seats while his father wiped down the wood. "I'm glad you pulled this out, Daed. It will be good to put this sleigh to use. You ought to attach some sleigh bells on the back for Mamm. She loves that."

Looking pleased, his father nodded. "She surely does at that. Hearing them ring through the fields will add a bit of Christmas cheer, too." Rubbing his hand along the back of the polished wood, he mused, "I have a feeling this old girl has been feeling sorely neglected. We've hardly gotten more than an inch of snow in the last three years."

"I was beginning to wonder if snowy winters were going to be in our past."

"I've thought the same, son. But this winter has showed us that ain't the case at all. Why, I am wondering if we'll see the ground again before March."

"I heard it's supposed to snow again tonight."

Daed grunted. "That means we're going to have some shoveling to do before church."

John Michael nodded. "I'll do it. I might walk over and see if I can help Grace King, too."

"Ah, yes. She's staying over at the Lees'." He straightened and carefully folded the cloth in his hands. "Your mother told me."

His father was a lot of things but subtle wasn't one of them. "I'm sure I told you, too, Daed."

"How was chatting with Grace after all this time?"

John Michael paused. "Difficult at first. She didn't seem to want anything to do with me."

"The sisters are close. No doubt there were some hard feelings there."

"There were." John Michael figured that was also an understatement. Grace's demeanor had bordered on arctic. "She eventually came around, though."

"That don't surprise me none," his father said with a new gleam in his eyes. "She always seemed to have a light within her that Beth didn't."

John Michael just about choked. "Daed, you can't say things like that."

"Whyever not?"

"It's not nice."

Daed waved a hand. "I'm not being mean if I think it's the truth. And I do."

"Still . . ."

"I always thought it interesting to see how two *kinner* from the same family could be so different. And those girls certainly are."

"Indeed."

"And while we would have loved Beth and appreciated her gifts . . ."

John Michael felt his lips twitch. This roundabout way of talking about a touchy subject was extremely familiar. "Just say it, Daed."

"Very well." After looking like he was bracing himself, he blurted, "If you and Grace one day found something between you, I wouldn't necessarily think it a bad thing."

"Don't start matchmaking."

"I'm not." His father's eyes twinkled. "One would have had to be deaf and blind not to notice the way Grace used to fancy you years ago. She would blush beet red every time you spoke a word to her."

He had noticed Grace's infatuation, but he'd tried not to dwell on it. She was too young for him, and he'd been determined to work things out with Beth. Later, when he was starting to realize that there was nothing between them except the sense that they should be perfect for each other, he'd begun to doubt his feelings for any woman.

He'd spent so much time with Grace because he was at the King household trying to connect with Beth. But more often than not, after he'd caught up on the day's events with Beth, they would start talking to her sisters—and he would end up talking mostly to Grace.

He'd felt at ease with Grace; enjoyed her company. She was quiet and liked to read, just like he did. She loved animals and had a goofy sense of humor. He also felt as if she needed him—as if she'd gotten lost in the shuffle of her boisterous household and needed someone to pay attention to her.

So he did.

But then one day when he was in the barn with her, looking at a new foal, he realized that he'd found everything he'd been searching for in Grace, instead of Beth.

He was horrified. Needing space from both women, he broke things off with Beth abruptly—and somehow managed to look like a cad to the whole family.

"Grace isn't blushing when she sees me now."

"Of course not," Daed said quickly. "She's a mature young woman with her own pet-sitting business. However, I have often wondered if feelings ever really change."

"Are you saying that you think Grace could still have a crush on me?"

"I'm only thinking of me and your mother, son. I met her when I was fifteen and we got married at eighteen. Both of our parents were so pleased; it was practically an arranged match. Then, through the years, she and I grew up, had you, raised sheep for a while, and farmed. Now we are almost retired, but still I love her." He scratched the back of his neck. "I love your mother, but sometimes I canna help but be amazed by the idea that two people can form a bond when they're children, adopt other interests, and after all this time still feel the same."

"Beth is happy now. Grace said she's interested in another man."

"Ah. Well, it has been several years."

"It's been three."

"Three years is a long time."

"It's a really long time when you're in your twenties. We're not going to get back together."

His father chuckled. "I weren't talking about Beth and you know it."

"Even if there was something between Grace and me, we couldn't pursue it. It would cause too much strain between her and her sister."

"Maybe. Or maybe if her sister was happy with someone else, she would understand."

"I don't know about that. Then there's her parents." Looking at his father, he said, "Remember how upset they were with me for breaking her heart?"

"I remember some angry words being said."

Mr. and Mrs. King had said some harsh words that weren't true, but he hadn't known how to defend himself. "Her parents would never allow me to call on Grace."

"Like I said, Grace ain't a young girl anymore. She has a mind of her own. So it seems to me it's not her parents' or her sister's opinions that you should be worried about."

"You've got a good point, Daed. If I now know one thing about Grace King, it's that she's a woman who knows her own mind. And she's gotten pretty good at speaking it, too."

# CHAPTER 10

"Snooze, I think you have more clothes than I do," Grace declared as she sat on the laundry room floor. The dog sat next to her and wagged his tail as she sorted through his many sweaters, jackets, and booties.

Holding up two tiny light-blue booties, each one with Velcro around the ankles and slip-resistant pads on the bottom, she giggled. "Do you actually wear such things?"

As if he could understand every word she said, Snooze raised his ears and tilted his head. He was looking so affronted, Grace imagined he was wondering why she thought light-blue booties were unnecessary for a fancy dog like himself.

Giggling again, she put the booties down and picked up a cozy-looking red fleece dog sweater. "Since we're only going for a short walk to get the mail, I don't think booties are needed. But it is awfully cold out." Holding up the sweater, she said, "How about this red sweater? What do you think?"

To her surprise, Snooze hopped right on her lap and easily moved his front paws into each tiny sleeve of the sweater. After she fastened the three snaps on his chest, he lifted his chin and barked.

Obviously, he liked his sweater very much!

"*Jah*, I agree. You look mighty handsome, sir," she said as she scratched his neck. "Let's go for a little walk, *jah*?"

Leaping off her lap, Snooze barked again and wagged his tail some more. He was also gazing at her with something close to happiness for the very first time.

Grace felt like she'd finally learned an important lesson. The way to one wiener dog's heart wasn't companionship and cuddles. It was sweaters and promised walks.

Feeling like they'd finally made some progress, she hooked on his black leash and led the dog to her snow boots and cloak. She put on both, and then finally wrapped a dark-green wool muffler around her *kapp* and black bonnet.

"We might look like a pair of overstuffed teddy bears, but we'll be warm enough, I think. Let's go."

After she opened the door, Snooze led the way down the front steps that she'd cleared of snow early that morning. At the end of their walk, she planned to pick up the mail.

The Lees had a long driveway that led out to the main road. It was at least a half-mile long, and it had a slight curve as it ventured down the hill toward the highway. Because of that, no one who drove by would see the house.

Grace imagined that the Lees had planned it that way. They'd even designed for the driveway to end in an arch at the front of the house. One could drive a buggy or a vehicle almost to the front door.

Dotted along both sides of the expanse were pear trees. When Grace visited in September, their leaves had just begun to turn golden yellow. Now the trees were bare, well, except for the thousands of white twinkling lights that had been strung on them.

The lights were on an automatic timer and when they'd first turned on, Grace gasped. It was such a magical sight.

She soon discovered that the long walk to get the mail with Snooze took easily double the time that it would've taken on her own. Snooze was a tiny dachshund with short legs. Then, too, he was a careful stepper, taking care not to walk on patches of ice.

As they continued on and the house faded into the distance, a flicker of worry settled in her insides. Maybe his little booties weren't so unnecessary after all.

"For a dog who ran off on his own and slept in straw, you seem mighty persnickety today."

Snooze didn't acknowledge her. He simply kept meandering on the drive, stopping often to paw in the snow.

When they finally reached the mailbox, she was glad she'd thought ahead and brought along the canvas tote. The Lees had received at least five catalogs and three times that many Christmas cards. As she carefully placed them all in her tote, she felt a pang of sadness, imagining all the cards at her own house.

Her mother often waited to open the cards until after supper. Then, by candlelight, each of the girls would take a turn opening the red and green envelopes and reading the personal messages carefully written inside.

When all of the day's cards had been opened and shared, they'd help their mother hang them up. By Christmas Eve, there would be cards strung everywhere, each one a visible reminder of their many relatives and friends.

Grace was now embarrassed that she'd always thought such a display was a bit too much.

Now she realized it wasn't too much at all.

They were how their family decorated for Christmas. And they weren't even just decorations, either. They were symbols of all of their many friends and family and how they all cared about each other.

Actually, all of it—the baking, the candles, her mother's excitement—it was all special. Why had it taken an absence from her house to enable her to realize how much all of those traditions meant to her?

When her family got back, Grace was going to tell her mother how much she liked and appreciated her efforts. Christmas really wasn't the same without those familiar touches.

For some reason, the cards, or lack of them, made her think of Miss Dorma again, and gave her a perfect idea. She could make some fudge and a homemade card and bring them over to her.

Maybe she could even think of some other people she could do that for.

Doing something nice like that would certainly be worth the cost of hiring the driver again.

Snooze, who'd been standing by her side and looking rather disgruntled, barked.

"I know. It's chilly out here. Don't worry, your quilt will be over you in no time." After walking him into the field for a while, where he pawed and sniffed and eventually did his business, they returned to the drive and headed back to the house.

"Ready to go back and make fudge, Snooze?"

She continued her one-sided conversation the entire way. She and the dog were making strides, if only small ones. Maybe by the end of her time with him he would realize that she could be a new friend.

She kind of doubted it, though.

Finally, after being gone almost an hour, they reached the front steps leading up to the door. "*Gut* job, Snooze," she said with a smile. "You got to wear your sweater, we had a nice walk, and even got the—"

Her voice caught in her throat as she noticed that the front door was ajar.

There were also new footprints in the snow, ones she knew without a doubt she hadn't made.

This time, Grace didn't hesitate or try to pretend that things were all right. She dropped the canvas tote on the walk, picked up a startled Snooze, and started running to John Michael's house.

Terrible, awful ideas ran through her head as she ran through the snowy fields and around the woods. Images about what could've happened if she'd been inside.

What could have happened if she'd been asleep?

Or sitting in the kitchen.

Or standing in the shower.

As each thought entered her head, she shivered violently. Fear building upon each fear until she was certain that she was never going to be able to relax again.

Her heart was pounding and she was gasping for breath by the time she came upon the edge of the Millers' property and passed the pile of straw where Snooze had been sleeping.

She kept running.

Just as she paused to scan the area, hoping to find either John Michael or one of his parents, the back door opened and he stepped out.

"Grace? Grace, what's wrong?" he asked as he ran toward her. He was in shirtsleeves, wool slacks, and suspenders. His feet were stuffed into brown work boots. It must have been hastily done because the laces were still loose.

He didn't have on a coat. Not even a hat on his head.

But he was there. Feeling incredibly relieved, she launched herself at him, with Snooze still trapped in her arms. "John Michael," she gasped, "I think someone is in the Lees' *haus*."

"Easy now," he murmured as his strong arms went around her. "My goodness. Your heart is beating like you ran a marathon."

"I feel like I have."

When she shivered again, he pulled her closer.

Only when Snooze grunted did he release her.

"Sorry, pup," Grace said as she carefully set him back down on the ground. When he whined and pulled from her grasp, she released his leash.

Realizing that wasn't safe, she turned to claim him again. But John Michael claimed her hand instead. "Don't worry about Snooze. He'll be all right."

Sure enough, the dog only walked toward a comfy chair on the covered porch. Right away, he hopped up on the cushion and curled into a snug ball, his leash hanging down.

"I guess he is all right," she said, feeling like there was a frog in her throat.

And just like that, all the worry and fear that had consumed her during her run to his house consumed her again. Unable to help herself, she started trembling.

"Oh, Grace." John Michael reached for her, again enfolding her safely into his arms. Though she knew she shouldn't, she leaned against him, taking comfort in his arms.

He ran one hand down the length of her back. "Are you all right? Did someone attack you at the house? Are you hurt?"

"*Nee.* Just scared." Taking a deep breath, she pulled away.

"Can you tell me what happened?"

"I took Snooze for a walk to get the mail," she replied, looking into his eyes. "It took a long time. Maybe an hour? When I got back to the house, I noticed fresh footprints." She swallowed, attempting to regain her composure. "That's when I noticed that the door was ajar."

His expression hardened. "What did you do then?"

"I dropped the mail, picked up Snooze, and ran here as fast as I could."

"You did the right thing."

"I wasn't even thinking," she admitted. "All I wanted to do was run. I was so scared." No, she was so very terrified.

Looking more disturbed by the second, John Michael leaned in closer as if he was trying to transfer some of his heat to her. "You're trembling. You must be cold. Let's get you and Snooze inside."

After taking a step, she paused in alarm. "Wait, John Michael. I can't go inside right now. I need to take care of the house."

"We will."

"But someone could be stealing all of Mr. and Mrs. Lee's things." Just imagining what they would say about that, she grabbed at his arm. "I have to do something."

"You are. You came here to safety and you found me."

"But—"

"We'll discuss it after we get you out of the cold," he said in a new tone that brooked no argument. "Come, now." He wrapped a steady arm around her shoulders and ushered her inside, calling Snooze to follow.

The moment he opened the door and they stepped across the threshold, she felt as if she'd entered another world. The older farmhouse was decorated rather sparsely, but everything was beautiful and finely made. There were cherry cabinets built into the living room wall. A gorgeous dining room table stood proudly in the middle of the dining room. It had a gold-and-silver woven table runner that ran along the center.

The walls were painted a creamy buttermilk. A lovely musical clock hung on the wall. So did an antique quilt with a dark ruby-red border.

But more than anything, she was taken in by the delicious scent that seemed to envelope every room. A combination of ginger-bread, vanilla, and evergreen. Everything that reminded her of Christmas and comfort.

It felt familiar and comforting. And inviting.

"Grace?" John's voice was hesitant behind her.

Belatedly, she realized she'd just been standing like a statue in the middle of the entryway. She hadn't even edged out from under his arm. Embarrassed, she stepped away. Tried to pretend that she wasn't feeling awkward. "Sorry. I, um, well, your home is mighty lovely."

He looked at her in confusion. "But you've been here before, yes? I mean, you've been here when we hosted church."

"I've been to your barn for church. Never inside." While it was true that a lot of women did venture into each other's homes, she hadn't felt comfortable doing that. Too much hurt from the past had lingered, and simply being around him had been hard.

"Ah. Yes. I suppose not." As if he was mentally shaking himself, he reached out to take her cloak.

She unfastened the button and handed it to him. After she set her black bonnet and scarf on the dining room table, she knelt down to see to Snooze.

She unhooked his leash and rubbed his head. He put up with the attention but pulled away when she attempted to remove his sweater. "I guess he wants to keep it on."

"No harm in that, Grace."

Getting back to her feet, she faced John again. "You're right. I guess that is true."

"Let's go into the kitchen. We'll talk there."

When she walked in, she noticed that there were three loaves of apple-cinnamon bread cooling on the counter. They looked and smelled heavenly. "Your *mamm* has been busy."

"*Jah.* She has." He smiled slightly. "My father often says that he thinks he can gain five pounds just from the scents of my mother's baking."

"Our *haus* is the same way."

He grinned. "Yes, it is. Your mother is a mighty fine cook. And a busy one!"

For the first time, the reminder that he used to spend time at her house didn't bring forth a flash of pain. "You're right. Um, actually, until I got to the Lees', I was always of the mind that my mother did too much. She is always making something or baking something or has some unfinished project lying on the table."

"You do come from a large family, Grace. There are a lot of girls to look after."

"There are. But it's just my *mamm*'s way, too. She doesn't like to sit still. And, I'm afraid, she's rather messy. My father sometimes picks up more than she does."

"I always thought it was sort of cute."

"Cute?"

"Well, you never had to worry about putting something out of place," he related. "There's a lot of comfort in that."

"I always took it for granted," Grace mused. "Now, though? . . . I would give a lot to be surrounded by her love."

"Oh, Grace." He guided her to a chair and then, to her surprise, crouched on his heels in front of her. "We need to call the sheriff."

Then he turned, got up, grabbed ahold of the phone that was hanging on the wall, and dialed.

She listened as he spoke and shared her news about the footprints and the house.

"Hold on," he said after a minute. Looking in her direction, he asked, "Do you want to meet them at the house or visit with them after they check things out?"

"Can I talk to them here?"

"*Jah.* I think that would be best." He relayed her wishes into the receiver. Then, after affirming his address, hung up. "I think they'll be here within the hour."

Her nerves crept up on her again. "What do we do in the meantime?"

"I'll get Snooze a little bowl of milk and we'll have tea, eat warm apple bread, and wait."

She clenched her hands in a tight knot in her lap and wondered what she and John Michael were going to discover at the house . . . and what could possibly happen next.

# CHAPTER 11

John Michael couldn't remember a time when he'd felt more useless. As he took a seat next to Grace while Sheriff Brewer pulled out a notebook, he felt like his hands were tied. Grace was frightened and nervous, but there was little he could do to help her. He couldn't make the upcoming conversation easier or offer any comfort. This was her story and he wasn't her man.

Besides, it had been obvious from the moment Sheriff Brewer arrived that he wanted to hear what happened from Grace and from her alone.

So, while Snooze was sleeping on a quilt next to the fireplace, John sat and listened to Grace tell her story to the sheriff. He sat a respectful ten inches away while her voice quavered and her skin turned pale again.

And made himself stay silent when it was obvious that she was feeling flustered and tongue-tied.

He'd done all that because he felt he had no choice. He wasn't anything to Grace. Not really a friend, not a confidant, not even a neighbor. He was simply a person who was nearby and was willing to help her.

That wasn't surprising.

What was surprising was how much he wished she felt differently.

After she told her story and answered a few more questions about the number of footprints and what direction they'd taken, she leaned forward. "Sheriff, please tell me what you discovered when you went to the house. Did you find the intruder?"

Sheriff Brewer darted a glance at John Michael before answering. "I'm sorry, Grace. We did not."

"Was he already gone?" John asked, unable to keep silent any longer.

"I'm not sure." Looking at Grace, he added, "Miss King, I went inside with one of my deputies, but I've gotta be honest with you. There wasn't any sign of anything having been disturbed."

Grace looked thoroughly confused. "But the door was open. And there were strange footprints. Someone was there."

The sheriff nodded. "We did find that the door was ajar. But there were no clear footprints. Instead, it looked like someone had walked around the yard a time or two. Or more than that."

"*Nee.* I saw new, distinct footprints." Sounding hurt, she said, "If you didn't see them, why did you ask me so much about them? Were you just pretending to believe me?"

"Now, don't get upset," the sheriff said, waving a hand like he was attempting to calm a feisty horse. "I wouldn't be here if I didn't want to hear what happened from you. All I'm doing is trying to put everything together."

"All right. Then you have to believe I did see those footprints and the door was definitely open."

Unable to help himself, John Michael spoke again. "She was really upset when she arrived here. Grace wouldn't have acted that way without reason."

She looked at him and smiled.

"I believe you. I believe you both. Now I'm going to take you back to the house and we're going to go through it again. Nothing looked disturbed, but there could easily be things missing that I couldn't know about."

Grace bit her bottom lip. "It's a mighty big *haus.* I don't know if I can tell what might have gone missing."

"Of course not. But you could check for some obvious things

that might be taken, right?" Sheriff Brewer asked patiently. "Things like artwork, electronics, and computers."

"All you can do is your best," John soothed as he moved closer to her. "Right?"

"I suppose so," Grace said.

"I think it's the best place to start. We can always contact Mr. and Mrs. Lee if you have any questions."

"They're going to be so upset if they've been robbed. What if they blame me?"

"I don't see why they would," Sheriff Brewer said.

"I know Parker and Cindy Lee. They're kind people," John Michael added. "All they're going to say is that they're glad you're all right."

"Do you really think so?"

"I know so. I've lived next to them for years. I promise, they're going to worry more about you and their dog than any objects in the house."

Looking calmer, Grace attempted to smile. "You are right. And Snooze is fine."

John Michael grinned at Snooze, who was now snoring softly. "Snooze is better than fine. He's been in *gut* hands."

Sheriff Brewer stood up. "Are you ready to go, Grace?"

She looked shaken up but determined. "I am," she said as she got to her feet. "Let me just go get Snooze."

"Tell me who Snooze is again?" Sheriff Brewer asked.

"He is the Lees' little dachshund," Grace replied. "That's why I'm staying at their house."

Grace hadn't looked to him, but John Michael didn't let that deter him from what he needed to do. "I'll go with you," he offered as she knelt down to pick up the sleepy dog.

As she reached for Snooze, she said, "I've already taken up so much of your time. There's no need for you to do that."

Not even caring that the sheriff was watching and listening to their conversation, John Michael stepped closer to her and curved a hand around her shoulder. "There's every need," he said gently. "I'm not going to let you walk in there until I know you feel safe."

Sheriff Brewer smiled. "Though I can promise you I'm not going to let anything happen to either you or Snooze, having a good friend with you might be a good idea."

John Michael stiffened, half waiting for Grace to point out that he wasn't her good friend. But instead, she simply smiled and nodded. "All right."

After he helped Grace put on her cloak and boots, he shrugged on a jacket and took Snooze in his arms so she wouldn't have to carry him around. Then they all piled in the sheriff's vehicle. John Michael knew he could either hitch a ride back home from the sheriff or simply walk.

None of them said much as the sheriff drove them to the Lees' house. Grace sat in the back seat with Snooze and John Michael sat up front with Sheriff Brewer.

When he turned onto the lane, John Michael felt the tension increase in the vehicle. Sheriff Brewer must have, too, because he slowed to a stop.

"Grace, how far away were you when you noticed that something wasn't right?" he asked. "This far?"

"Oh, *nee.* I didn't notice anything until I was almost at the door."

"I'm going to drive slowly up. You look around and tell me if you see anything different or out of the ordinary."

"I will do that."

When they were almost to the circular drive, she called out. "I was standing about right here when I noticed the door was ajar."

"Let's park here, then."

They all got out. Snooze wagged his tail, looking pleased to be back somewhere familiar. He was pulling on his leash toward the house.

"I'll keep track of him, Grace," John said easily. "You concentrate on describing what you saw to Sheriff Brewer."

The sheriff had his notebook out again. "Take your time."

Grace stepped forward, then gasped. "The footprints were not like this."

John Michael eyed the area where she was pointing. The path looked exactly like the sheriff had described. All that he could see was evidence that someone—or a group of people—had walked all over the area.

"This is how it looked when we arrived," the sheriff said.

"Would someone have wiped out their footsteps on purpose?" John asked. "Like, in order to hide their prints?"

"Possibly." There was a note of skepticism in the sheriff's voice, though.

Grace inhaled sharply but didn't argue. Only turned to the front door. "It was open."

"We closed it after we left." Sheriff Brewer walked to the door and opened it to where a small piece of tape was on the entryway floor. "This is how far apart it was when we got here. Was this about what it looked like?" Sheriff Brewer asked.

She tilted her head to one side, trying to remember. "Maybe . . . At first I thought the door was closed. Only after I was on the steps did I realize that it had been opened."

"Are you ready to go inside and look around now?"

She hesitated. "I think so."

John Michael walked to her side. "I'll be right beside you," he said as he picked up Snooze.

After glancing at the sheriff again, Grace walked inside, John Michael following close behind.

Though he had just been in the house, he hadn't noticed much besides Grace. Now he looked around with interest, hoping to spy something new. But it looked much the same as it always had. Clean and tidy. Overwhelmingly big.

When Snooze squirmed, he leaned over to place the dog on the floor. John decided to keep a loose hold on his leash since the front door was still open.

"Do you see anything out of order?" the sheriff asked.

"*Nee.* Though . . ." Bending down, she pressed two fingers to the marble floor. "This is different."

"What is?" Sheriff Brewer had out his cell phone and looked ready to take a picture.

"It's too clean."

"How can you tell?"

"I take Snooze in and out this door several times a day. I make sure to pull my boots on and off whenever I go in and out, but Snooze's tiny paws are harder to keep clean. After the first day, I gave up on trying to keep the floor scrubbed. I decided I would just mop it every couple of days. I washed it yesterday morning, but after last night and this morning, this whole area was covered again with tiny tracks." Getting back to her feet again, she said, "I can promise you that someone wiped the floor."

Sheriff Brewer took a picture of the marble floor and wrote down some notes. "All right. That's a start. Now—"

Suddenly, Snooze started barking and whining, then pulled out of John Michael's grasp and tore down the hall.

# CHAPTER 12

S nooze. Oh, *nee*, Snooze! You leave that mouse alone."

Snooze didn't even think about minding her. Right before her eyes, the tiny dachshund turned into a wild animal and attacked the mouse it had cornered with glee.

John Michael ran forward, but he wasn't quick enough.

Within seconds, the pale gray mouse was hanging limp from Snooze's mouth. Its tiny black eyes frozen open.

Grace felt kind of sick. "Snooze, you drop that *meisli* right now."

He did not. Instead, Snooze stared at her like she was asking something crazy. His tail was wagging and he looked pleased as punch. Rather proud, too.

She would have chuckled if the sight wasn't so gruesome.

"I think that *hund* needs a new name. Maybe Trouble instead of Snooze," John Michael said as he joined her. "He gets into more trouble than most dogs I know who are double his size."

"He's a fierce hunter, for sure and for certain," Sheriff Brewer murmured.

Still staring at the dead mouse, she said, "Would one of you please help me dispose of that creature?"

John Michael stepped forward and pointed a finger at Snooze. "Drop it."

The dog whined but dutifully tossed the mouse on the ground.

Sheriff Brewer pulled out a plastic bag from a hidden pocket in his uniform and scooped it up. After he knotted the bag, he looked at Grace and chuckled. "I'm not going to lie, that dog had

me going for a moment. I thought he found a dead body or something."

Now that the mini-crisis was solved, Grace felt herself smile,
too. "I thought it was something worse as well." Turning to
Snooze, she said, "I don't know what to do with you. Killing mice
ain't *gut*."

"If Snooze hadn't gotten it, it would be living with you the rest of
the week," John Michael pointed out. "I think he helped you out."

Imagining how restless she'd be, constantly wondering where
the mouse was, she sighed. "You are right. That would be awful."

"I'll throw this outside as I leave, Grace," Sheriff Brewer said.

"No, wait," Grace said. "I haven't looked for missing items yet."

"Yes, we'll need to take a tour and look around. But before we
do that, I have a question for you."

*"Jah?"*

"Did you lock the door before you walked down to get the mail?"
The sheriff's question made her pause. *"Nee."*

"There was a bit of a wind earlier today. It's just a guess, but I
have a feeling that maybe the latch didn't close all the way before
you walked out. That happens from time to time. The wind could
have popped the door open."

Her face began to heat. He didn't believe her. He thought she'd
imagined the footprints in the snow, hadn't shut the front door
firmly behind her, and was the type of woman to get hysterical
around mice or anything else.

Okay, she might be scared of mice . . . but she would never have
made a fuss about the door and footprints unless she'd been sure
something was off.

She inhaled, planning to let him know that he had gotten
things wrong.

John Michael pressed one of his hands lightly on her back.
"Let's go look around, Grace."

She nodded and started leading the men and a disgruntled
Snooze through the rooms. After ten minutes she said, "It all
looks fine. Nothing is out of place."

"That's a good thing," the sheriff said lightly. "Let's finish up, though."

The rest of the house looked just as pristine. By the time they returned to the front entryway, Grace was feeling disheartened, and embarrassed, too.

She didn't think she'd imagined that something had been wrong . . . but what if she had? Maybe the sheriff had been right.

"Do you want to look anyplace else, Grace?" Sheriff Brewer asked.

Feeling glum, she shook her head.

John Michael stepped in front of her. "I sure appreciate you coming out when we called, Sheriff." He held out his hand and shook the other man's hand.

"You're welcome. That's what we're here for." Leaning down a bit so he could look her in the eyes, Sheriff Brewer said, "Don't hesitate to contact us if you see anything else suspicious."

Suddenly wanting him out of the house, she smiled tightly. "*Danke*. I will do that."

As she watched the sheriff slip on the jacket he'd taken off soon after they first walked inside, Grace attempted to get her emotions back in check. But it was futile. She felt near tears. The best she could do was to keep calm until the men left. Then, when the door closed and she was all alone, she could fall apart.

"Here's my card, Grace. Hopefully you won't need it, but don't be shy, now." He smiled then. "And Merry Christmas."

Holding the card tightly in her right hand, she nodded. "Merry Christmas, Sheriff."

"John Michael, do you want a ride back to your house?"

Turning to look at Grace, John shook his head. She looked upset and frustrated. There was no way he was going to leave her alone to worry all by herself. "No, thanks. I think I'll stay here for a bit and make sure everything is locked up tight." He winked. "I'll be on the lookout for more mice, too."

The sheriff laughed as he picked up the bag as promised.

"Sounds good, though my money would be on that dog to hunt them out." After giving a little salute, Sheriff Brewer walked back out to his vehicle.

When he was halfway there, Grace shut the door with a sigh. Then she turned around and leaned against it. "Well, that was a waste of time. He didn't believe me."

"Maybe it wasn't that he didn't believe you . . ." His voice drifted off. Truly, what could he say? It was obvious that the sheriff thought Grace had gotten a touch of nerves and let her imagination run away with her.

She smiled grimly. "Don't worry about trying to find a better, easier way to describe the situation. There isn't a better one. Sheriff Brewer didn't believe me."

"For what it's worth, I actually hope that it was nothing. I'd love it if we were to discover that the door did accidentally get blown open."

She raised an eyebrow. "So you hope I did let my imagination run wild?"

"I don't want you to be in danger, Grace," he corrected, meaning that sincerely.

She slumped. "I know what you meant, but there really were fresh footprints. I *know* there were."

Looking into her eyes, he realized she was blessing him with pure honesty. But what he saw there was a vulnerability he hadn't realized she was capable of. It affected him like a punch to the chest. "Are you scared about staying here alone?" he asked gently. "I'm back on call tomorrow morning. But, if you want, I could stay here."

"Overnight?" Her voice came out almost as a squeak.

"Well, *jah*." Though he thought it was understood, he gave her the words. "Of course, I'll sleep on the couch or in one of the spare bedrooms. I would never take advantage of you."

"I know you wouldn't, John Michael. I thank you for the offer, but I'll be fine."

"If you'd rather, I could ask my mother to come over."

She chuckled. "I don't think that would make things easier. There's no telling what she and I would talk about."

Since his mother was a talker, he could only imagine. "If you want to stay alone, will you at least write down our phone number? You could call if you hear something suspicious."

She walked to the kitchen counter and pulled out a notepad and pencil. "*Danke*. That would ease my mind."

He took the pencil from her and wrote down two numbers— his home phone number and his cell phone number.

"You have a cell phone?"

"I use it at work."

"Oh." She nodded. "*Jah*, I guess you would need to have it for firefighting. You have a very important job."

He had always believed that he did. He was proud of being a firefighter. Proud of the work they did in the community. Proud of his ability to do something demanding that stretched him to his limits. When he was called out, when he was on one of the trucks, he felt like he was at his best. His mind was clearer, his senses sharper. His body was tense, ready to go into action, to put all the hard work and training he had acquired to good use.

And yes, he did save lives. It was important.

But as he looked at Grace, he knew that it wasn't more important than her needs.

"Don't hesitate to call me, Grace. If you even suspect someone is outside or you start to feel scared, you call me."

She blinked at his high-handed request.

He cleared his throat, ready to argue with her.

But instead, she nodded. "I will."

"Okay, then. I had better go."

"*Jah*. Don't worry about me. I'm going to do a little bit of baking. And Snooze is worn out. Neither of us will leave except for a quick break outside."

He pulled on his coat and walked to the door. "Don't forget to lock up."

"Be careful tomorrow, John Michael. May God be with you."

He smiled his thanks before turning and heading out.

After he heard the dead bolt click into place, he started walking. For the first time in days, the sky was clear. There wasn't a chance of snow. Everything was calm.

He hoped and prayed everything would stay that way.

# CHAPTER 13

Dawn broke early the next morning, carrying with it a beautiful sunrise and clear skies. Rays of sunlight glinted through the breakfast room's windows, creating patterns of bright squares along the wooden floor. Snooze, once again back to form, was entertaining himself by stretching out in the various sunny spots and napping.

As Grace sipped her third cup of coffee, she felt jealous. Unlike the dog, who seemed to have picked up no lasting effects from either the break-in scare or the mouse, she was spent and exhausted.

Maybe even more than that.

After John Michael left the night before, she had felt so alone it was almost terrifying. Never in her life had anything prepared her for what had happened that day.

What was still happening. She was not only having to come to terms with the fact that she had seen tracks outside her door, but they'd been purposefully removed, too. They'd also opened the door, and then left without a trace.

All of this was scary. But it was compounded by the fact that her family was out of town. If they hadn't been, she would have run right home.

Her parents would have helped her, too. Daed would have dropped everything and inspected the house with her. He wouldn't have acted impatient or doubtful, either. Instead, he would have walked around until they both felt that everything was safe and sound.

And her mother would have been so comforting! Mamm would have given her a hug and talked her through all her fears. Even her sisters would have stayed with her, or at the very least, would have made her laugh and relax a bit.

Her best friend, Jennifer, would have helped her, too.

Just as John Michael had.

The realization hit her hard. She'd been sure she couldn't trust him, shouldn't rely on him—but again and again, he was proving her to be wrong.

Here she'd thought their relationship was confusing, but maybe it was only her feelings for him that were.

Last night she'd been so bewildered about her feelings for John Michael and worried about the prowlers returning that she'd paced and fretted. She walked the halls of the large house with a flashlight in her hand and peered into the five other bedrooms at regular intervals. Her imagination ran wild. Sometimes she was even afraid that she was going to suddenly see a stranger reclining on one of the beds and waiting for her when she peeked in.

She didn't drift off to sleep until long after midnight, only to find herself wide awake just after three in the morning. Her body felt tense and charged, as if she'd been on the receiving end of some kind of foreign electrical current; her legs were restless and she felt like she was burning up. Thirty minutes after that, she was freezing.

She ended up making cinnamon scones around four in the morning. Only after she'd taken them out of the oven and the whole first floor smelled of sugar and spices did she get tired again.

She'd returned to bed and fell into an exhausted slumber. Consequently, she woke up later than usual and felt out of sorts.

After she finished that third cup of coffee, Grace knew she had to do something else besides worry and wander the halls.

When she spied the pan of scones that she'd made earlier that morning, she knew exactly what she needed to do. It was time to think about someone else for a change.

After carefully wrapping each cinnamon scone in waxed paper

and then placing them in a cardboard box, Grace decided to walk to see Miss Schultz.

She had considered taking Snooze for about a minute or two. Long enough to imagine Snooze being uncomfortable in the snow or squirming in her arms. Both of those things would only make him more disagreeable.

After taking him outside, giving him a generous portion of kibble, and attempting to pet his head, which he burrowed under his quilt so she couldn't pet him twice, Grace went on her way.

The moment she locked the door and started down the drive, her heart felt lighter. This was what she'd needed. Space from the worry of the Lees' house.

Though it was still cold, the day was still sunny and looked to stay that way. She had on sturdy boots, her cloak over her navy dress, and a red wool scarf and matching mittens. On her head was a black bonnet. It covered her hair and *kapp* and kept her ears warm. She was toasty warm and happy to be out walking.

She even had company. Blue jays, orioles, and cardinals were enjoying the sunny day, too. They chirped on the bare trees lining either side of both the driveway and the main road. Their antics made her laugh as she watched their aerial acrobatics.

An hour later, Grace felt refreshed and was knocking on Miss Schultz's door.

Checking from the side of the door, through a sheer fabric lining the window, Miss Schultz peered suspiciously at her. *"Jah?"*

"Miss Schultz? It's Grace King."

Faded gray eyes stared back at her. "Who?"

"Grace, Miss Schultz. I would see you at church and sometimes you'd let me sit with you." Smiling softly, she continued. "One time, you gave me a pen to draw with, but the ink inside of it burst and you and I got blue ink all over our hands! *Mei mamm* got mad at me, but you just laughed."

"Did I? Hmm."

Grace's spirits sank as she realized that Miss Dorma had no

memories of either the incident or of her. "It's okay if you don't remember," she said softly. "You were kind to many *kinner.*"

After staring again, Dorma said, "What do you want?"

Grace held up her cardboard box. "I brought you some scones."

"I don't want any."

The answer made Grace ache and feel a bit despondent. Maybe this visit wasn't doing any good and was only making Miss Dorma agitated.

But then she remembered her conversation with John Michael. Miss Schultz wasn't the woman she used to be. Maybe she'd even turned into someone she'd never been. And if that was the case? . . . their past didn't really matter. What did matter was the relationship they could form now.

Trying to look cheerful, she said, "I promise you will like them. May I come in? I'll put one on a plate for you."

Miss Schultz opened the door a crack but didn't step away so Grace could enter. It was almost as if she wasn't sure what to do next.

With a start, Grace realized that Miss Dorma wasn't used to having visitors. That realization made her so sad. Where was the woman's family? For that matter, how come their very own church community had forsaken her?

Grace had always loved her Amish faith. She believed her religion and chosen way of life encouraged the best in each person. Its basic principles were so simple, too: honoring God, love of family and friends, and respecting their traditions. It also emphasized the belief in helping out each other and being self-reliant. Though it wasn't the norm for members of their faith to send parents or grandparents to nursing homes, it *was* completely out of the ordinary to abandon someone when they needed help.

Just as Grace was feeling rather full of herself, she was brought up short. She was no better than anyone else. Whatever had happened with Dorma had happened and couldn't be changed. All

that could be changed was the future, which she could do something about.

She felt as though God was whispering in her ear, reminding
her that He had put Dorma Schultz in her path for a reason.

After waiting another half a minute, Miss Schultz made her
decision. She turned and walked inside, leaving the front door
open that small crack.

Taking a deep breath, Grace followed her inside. When she shut
the door behind her, she felt as if she had just entered a maze and
now she was off on a journey that she wasn't sure where it was
going to lead to.

"I'm watching the birds," Miss Schultz announced.

Entering the living room where the older lady was sitting,
looking vacantly out the window, Grace could hardly contain her
shudder. The house was filthy. Papers and unopened mail littered
every surface and table. Old tissues and napkins had been discarded on the floor. But that was not the extent of it. Dust clung to
the battery-operated lamp and the woodwork. She spied spider-
webs distended from the window frames.

But the worst of it was the smell that permeated the entire
room. The scents of an unwashed body, soiled clothes, all mixed
with urine and other things she wasn't sure she wanted to know,
filled the air. It was more than obvious that no one had cleaned
this house for a very long time.

She felt a lump in her throat that she wondered if she was ever
going to be able to dislodge. "Would you like a nice cup of tea and
the treat I brought?"

"*Jah.*"

Grace walked toward the kitchen and saw the mess that she
had almost expected. Dirty dishes were in the sink and on the
countertops. Food that had been left out unattended was either
dried up or forming mold.

But the worst part for Grace was seeing the new bottle of dish
soap standing idle by the sink. Someone had paid for the soap but
hadn't cared enough to wash the dishes for Miss Schultz.

Who on earth was letting her live like this?

"I'm just going to tidy up a bit," she called out, hoping that she sounded more merry than she felt. "You just watch the birds."

Miss Schultz didn't answer.

For the moment, Grace was pleased about that. Because she didn't think she would be able to form a coherent conversation. Her heart felt too heavy.

For the next forty minutes, Grace washed dishes, gathered trash, and scrubbed countertops. Little by little, in the kitchen, at least, the scent of lemon dish soap began to fill the air. It gave her an immense feeling of satisfaction. When the sink was sparkling and all of the dishes were put away, she scrubbed out the tea-kettle and set it to heat. Tried to be thankful that someone had paid the gas bills, because there had been no shortage of hot water and the range turned on immediately.

Then she searched the cupboards for tea. She found a surprising selection of tea and coffee. She was again reminded that someone had been seeing to the grocery shopping and had put everything away, but had not taken the next step to make sure Miss Schultz actually had decent meals to consume.

After steeping a cup of chamomile tea, she put a scone on the plate and carried it to Miss Schultz. "Here you go. I'm sorry it took me so long."

Miss Schultz eagerly took the tea from her and sipped.

"Careful, it's hot," she warned. Thank goodness she hadn't allowed the water to get too hot.

Miss Schultz ignored the fork and took a large bite of the scone. Her eyes widened, then she took another bite. The look on her face was priceless. It was obvious that she was enjoying it very much.

"Would you like another?"

"Jah."

Grace fetched another scone. Then got herself a cup of tea, too, needing something to warm her up. "Here you go."

Miss Schultz took a bite, then carefully set it down on her plate. Then stared hard at Grace. "You were always far too quiet."

Grace burst into laughter. "You do remember me! You're right. I always had my nose in a book, much to my teachers' dismay. I often got in trouble for reading a library book instead of my assignments."

Miss Schultz continued to study her. "*Jah*, you were a reader, but I still remember seeing ya whisper to your girlfriends or make eyes at the young men from time to time."

"I can't deny that." Of course, she'd really only been staring at one man—John Michael. Holding out a hand, she said, "I'm glad you remember me. My name is Grace," she said again.

"Grace."

"Grace King." Miss Schultz took another bite of her scone, then set it down and went back to staring at the birds. "Who takes care of you, Miss Schultz?"

"*Mei nohma* is Dorma. You may call me that."

"*Danke*, Dorma." Trying again, Grace asked, "Who comes in to cook and clean and shop for you?"

"I don't know."

"What do you mean? Did you forget their names? Or is it your family?"

"I don't have my family any longer. They moved away."

"Far away?"

Looking strangely coherent, Dorma Schultz stared directly at her. "Does it matter how far they are if they don't come here?"

Feeling tears prick her eyes, Grace shook her head. Then she remained sitting by Dorma Schultz's side and wondered what she should do next. For some reason only He knew.

The Lord had brought her to Dorma's side. Now she needed to help Dorma and make Him pleased with her efforts.

# CHAPTER 14

John Michael had just taken a bite of Hank's lasagna when the alarm bells started ringing throughout the fire station.

Immediately, John got to his feet, taking only the briefest of moments to look longingly at his tasty supper. With any luck, it would still be sitting there when he returned.

He raced down the stairs, Anderson at his heels. Trained well, they didn't speak, each intent on listening to the description of the call from their earpieces.

There was another fire. This time, it was out by the old abandoned VFW lodge. Unlike the previous time, this fire had broken out in an abandoned building within shouting distance of a popular Englisher neighborhood. The good news about that piece of information was that they wouldn't have to bring the pumper truck. They could hook up to a fire hydrant. The bad news, of course, was that they were going to have to be worried about the many homes nearby.

Once he got into the garage, he went to his turnout gear. First, he put on his hood, which he'd laid on top of his boots, then methodically stepped into the specially fitted uniform, all of it designed for his measurements, from his boot size to the breadth of his shoulders. Finally, he donned his helmet and SCBA, his self-contained breathing apparatus. He stuffed his gloves into a pocket so they were ready to be put on when he got closer to the destination.

"Captain," John acknowledged, then hopped up behind Anderson just as Hank got into the driver's seat and Cap jumped in by his side. Then, with lights flashing, they were off.

They each had a job to do. His, being the junior member of the trio, was to do whatever the captain told him to. But now, part of the department for a good while already, his body worked its usual routine. Checked gages, ran tests, and mentally prepared for what was to come.

Eight minutes later, Hank pulled to a stop in front of the burning building. Anderson hopped out and motioned for John Michael to assist with hooking up the hoses to the nearby fire hydrant.

After the hose was attached, Captain took the lead and began to spray the fire. Soon John Michael was by his side. He was aware of little beyond the captain's orders and the knowledge that Hank was breaking windows and ventilating the roof to make sure no stray gases were enclosed in air pockets.

A few moments later, the fire began to already look noticeably less ferocious. Less than ten minutes later, it was completely extinguished and the captain was motioning for John to disconnect his hose and for Hank to follow him closer to the smoking building.

By this time, Chief Nolan had arrived. He was dressed in full bunker gear, too, but it was obvious that he was letting Captain Butler take the lead.

When the scene was deemed safe, the captain motioned that they could all disengage their SCBA gear and lift up the shields on their helmets.

"You did good, John," Anderson said.

"Thanks. I'm glad the fire didn't spread."

"Yeah. Me, too."

John Michael noticed Anderson was frowning and watching their captain talk to both the chief and Sheriff Brewer, who had just pulled up. They were standing next to a small crowd of bystanders. From the snippets of conversations that were floating toward him, it was becoming obvious that the start of the fire was a mystery. The building had been out of use for at least two years and no one could remember a time when they'd seen a single person even stop in the VFW's parking lot.

"Something's going on," Anderson said. "Look how the sheriff's pointing to the subdivision."

"I wonder why he's doing that," John Michael said.

Just then Hank walked toward them. "Clean up the hoses," he called out to John Michael. "Anderson, come over here."

John felt a moment of envy. He didn't often mind being the rookie on the team, but it was moments like this, when his curiosity was strong, that he wished he could be in the midst of the conversations instead of doing the grunt work.

Just as quickly, he shook off the selfish thought. He had an important job to do and it was one he needed to do well. He went back to his tasks while the captain and chief inspected the site and Hank and Anderson spoke to the bystanders. Then the building inspection began. John Michael knew one or both of them would stay behind with the chief to finish the job while he rode back to the house with the captain.

An hour later, after they got back to the station, John Michael finally got the whole story from Captain Butler. Two houses in the neighborhood were robbed while the fire was going on. This same thing had happened in the north part of the county with another department. The sheriff and chief were beginning to think that some criminals now had a pattern. They were setting fire to an abandoned building or structure near occupied houses. Then, while everyone's attention was on the fire, they were breaking into houses, essentially undetected.

"This is terrible," John Michael said. "I hope they have an idea of who it was."

Captain Butler shrugged. "I don't think they do. Not yet, anyway."

Sean walked up and joined them. "I'm guessing some teenagers are doing it. They're always looking for a few kicks."

"At least no one was in the building. Someone in our homeless population could have been sleeping there."

"It's a blessing that no one was hurt, but it's a shame about that building," John Michael murmured. The building was at least a hundred years old and had once been both the high school and the county library. He'd always hoped someone with a lot of time and money could return it to its former glory.

"I agree completely." The captain slapped him on the back. "Since we can't go investigate, let's check out the truck and clean it up good. I don't want the salt on the roads to wreak havoc."

"Yes, sir," Sean said.

"Check your equipment good, too, Miller. That fire was a scorcher."

"Yes, Captain."

After examining and cleaning up his turnout gear, then putting it neatly away, he climbed into the truck and began going through the checklist.

Sean helped him clean the truck. Eventually, Anderson and Hank returned to the station and they joined the other men with the cleanup.

Conversation turned from work to their favorite nighttime topic: dinner.

John Michael was just wondering if there was going to be any lasagna left when Anderson walked to his side. "Hey, John Michael, did you happen to notice the pair of men standing off to the side when we left?"

"*Nee.* I mean, no. What about 'em?" he asked as he pulled out a rag and began wiping down the side panel, rubbing hard until the chrome shone.

"They seemed a little too interested."

John paused. "Did they? Do you think they started it?" He knew firebugs loved to watch the fruits of their labor.

"Maybe."

"Did you tell anyone?"

"Nah."

When John Michael first started, he would have been shocked or asked why. But now he knew how uncomfortable it was to be the one person making a mountain out of nothing. "Lots of men and women simply like to watch."

Anderson nodded. "That's true. Lots of guys simply like to stand around and watch," he repeated, seeming to find comfort in that.

John Michael stared at him in confusion but said nothing. Anderson was an experienced firefighter and would know if he needed to report his suspicions or not. When it was obvious Anderson wasn't going to say anymore on the subject, John attempted to lighten the mood. "Guess what? My mother's bringing by breakfast in the morning."

"No way. Really?"

"*Jah*. Two trays of cinnamon rolls." His mother was a fantastic cook and loved how much the other firemen appreciated her efforts. About once a month, she'd bring by either supper or breakfast. After John Michael realized that she wasn't bringing food to check up on him, he'd been pleased as punch about her visits.

Anderson grinned. "I love your *mamm*."

John Michael chuckled at the other man using the Amish word for *mom*. "I'll pass that on to her. She'll be right pleased."

"No need for that. I'll tell her myself in the morning," he said with a wink. "What time is she planning to stop by?"

"She said she'd be here by five."

"Perfect. If we aren't called out, we'll have plenty of time to eat before the new crew arrives."

As John Michael continued to wipe down the ladder truck, he prayed that was going to be the case.

But since it was December? That was doubtful. December, with the space heaters, lit candles, dry Christmas trees, and bad weather, meant that it was almost a certainty that they'd be called out again before his mother's rolls arrived.

Maybe even several times.

# CHAPTER 15

Grace had told herself that she was only making beef enchiladas because it was cold outside and a warm meal sounded wonderful. In addition, making a big meal for one person meant there would be lots of leftovers in the refrigerator. That would make her life easier, for sure and for certain.

All those things had been true, but as she looked around a kitchen that was slowly beginning to feel as comfortable as her own, Grace knew she hadn't been telling herself the truth.

No, the truth was that she was looking forward to John Michael's promise about stopping by that afternoon and she wanted to greet him with something warm and welcoming in the kitchen.

As she chopped up the last of the onion and placed it in the pan to cook with the oil, garlic, and hamburger, she couldn't help but imagine the look of surprise and pleasure on his face when he realized that she'd made a meal for them to share. That would make her so happy. Hadn't her mother often reminded her that the very act of cooking for another person was an act of love?

And while she might not be *in love* with John Michael Miller, she was fond of him.

She could practically hear her youngest sister, Sylvia, call out "liar, liar pants on fire."

"All right, Sylvia," she said to the empty room. "I'm something more than *just* fond of John Michael. I'm *mighty* fond of him. And don't you go complaining about that, because there is a difference."

Snooze, who'd been sleeping on a rug nearby, looked around the room and barked.

"Sorry, pup. It's just me being silly."

Ack! Now she was calling herself John Michael's pet name. Honestly, what was wrong with her?

Why, John Michael was most likely stopping by because of a sense of obligation. Would her supper give him the wrong impression?

*Nee.* Of course not. It was just supper.

But . . . what if his mother had also spoken about cooking as an act of love? Imagining the scene, she groaned. What if John Michael saw these enchiladas as an unwelcome sign of devotion? What if he thought she wanted to be something more than friends? He'd be mighty uncomfortable then.

And it would be a mighty good assumption, too, she told herself. Because she was kind of afraid that he would be right.

Her heart sank. This was why she needed her siblings around. Sylvia and Leona would say she was trying too hard. Her brothers would say she was making up a bunch of stuff and nonsense about a dish of food.

And Beth?

Well, Beth would be just plain mad.

Grace groaned again. What was she doing, being so forward? And what would he say if she was ever brave enough to share that she wasn't just "mighty fond" of him but that it had wandered into "like very much" territory?

Panic set in. Worse . . . how would she ever explain her change of heart to her mother? Ack . . . to Beth? Beth would likely never forgive her. And if Beth and Mamm united in their feelings, then her other sisters' opinions would follow. And the boys and Daed would distance themselves until the household grew calm again.

She'd have a terrible problem on her hands!

The doorbell chimed, interrupting her stewing. Thank the Lord!

Hurrying to the door, Snooze barking at her heels, she peeked outside and was pleased to see that the object of her thoughts was on her doorstep. Well, Snooze's doorstep.

"Hiya," Grace said as John Michael entered. "Look at you, you're still in your fireman's uniform and jacket."

He looked down at his clothing like he'd forgotten what he had on. "So I am."

She smiled at him. He looked as handsome and strong as ever. And he was looking at her like he was as delighted to be near her as she was to see him. Maybe he wouldn't mind that she cooked for him after all.

"How are you?" And, yes, her voice sounded a little raspy. Maybe a lot raspy.

"I'm better now," John Michael said as he shrugged off his jacket and hung it on a hook by the door.

As she continued to smile at him, he knelt on one knee to untie his boots and scratch Snooze behind his ears. "What smells . . . wait, is something burning?"

"Ack!" She turned and ran toward the kitchen, then stopped in her tracks when she realized that the pan was on fire. "Oh, no!" she cried. Just as she was about to run to the sink to fill up a pitcher with water, he stopped her.

"Never put water on a grease fire," he said as he grabbed a pan's lid and covered the flames. "Get some flour. Now."

She did as he asked, then watched in amazement as he grabbed a towel, pulled the pan off the burner, and then dumped a cupful of flour on the last of the flames.

With a couple of sputters and starts, the fire died, leaving in its place a burnt flour-laden meat dish. It was a mess.

A terrible, smelly, awful-looking mess.

Food was love, indeed!

Still calmly facing the range, John Michael turned the burner off and then wiped his hands on the dishtowel that she'd left next to the burner. A dishtowel that could've very well caught on fire if John Michael hadn't acted so quickly.

Grace realized then that she was panting. "I . . . I canna believe I was so careless!"

"Hush, now," he soothed, stepping closer to her. "It's all over."

She couldn't stop staring at the burnt contents of the pot. "John, I could've set the house on fire."

"But you didn't, Silly."

She was so upset, she didn't even care that he was calling her Silly. "Only because you were here."

"Then it's a blessing that I stopped by," he said lightly. "Ain't so?"

Grace heard everything he was saying. She was grateful for how calm and sweet he was being. But perversely, she kind of wanted him to act flustered, too. "John, I left that dishcloth right by the burner. It could have gone up in flames."

"But it did not," he repeated. "Now, stop worrying so much. That's why it's called an accident, *jah?*"

She couldn't believe he was actually making a small joke about what she'd done! "Yes, but I know better than to leave a pan on the cooktop unattended. I was acting so stupid." Because she'd been mooning about him. Imagining the worst, she continued. "I almost burned the Lees' *haus* down! Snooze could have died."

His expression softened. "Oh, Grace. Come here." He held out his arms.

Before she gave herself time to think twice about it, she walked into his arms. He was bigger than she. Taller. Wider, so much stronger. And at that moment, with her head against his shoulder and feeling his arms around her, Grace knew there was nowhere she would rather be.

It had been such a stressful, terrible couple of days. Being here all alone. Losing and then finding Snooze. Reacquainting herself with John Michael—and all the mixed-up emotions that entailed.

He rubbed her back with one hand. "Don't cry," he murmured softly. "There's no reason to cry."

Releasing a ragged sigh, she murmured. "God brought you here at just the right time. I'm so thankful for that."

"Me, too." He held her for another moment. She relaxed against him, loving how warm and solid he felt.

After another few minutes, Grace pulled away from him. She ducked her head in embarrassment. She probably should never have relaxed against him for so long.

"Grace? You okay?"

"What? Oh, *jah*." She pointed to the pan. "I was just thinking about that frying pan. I don't think it can be saved, do you?"

"We can pour out the food and look at it, but I think you are probably right." He picked it up. "Let's take it to the sink and see."

No way did she want him putting out her fire and washing up the mess, too. "*Nee*, I can do it."

"I'm a fireman. I can handle this," he said with a wink.

She still stayed by his side. Examining the pan after they threw the contents out. It was a stainless steel pan, but it had a thick black scar on its surface. It didn't look anything like Cindy Lee's other pots and pans. "If this was my own, I would maybe try to make it right. But I'm going to have to tell the Lees and pay for a new one."

He nodded. "I fear you are right." After a moment, he said, "I don't want to lecture you, but, Silly, please be careful when you're all alone."

"I am. I . . . I just forgot."

The smile that was playing on the corners of his lips stilled. "Hey. Wait a minute. Are those tears in your eyes? Are you crying?"

"*Nee*. Of course not."

He reached out and squeezed her hand. "We've known each other too long to start lying. Ain't so?"

That phrase, along with the truth of his words, made her swallow her pride. "All right. You called me *Silly*."

His eyes widened. "Why would that upset you?"

"I've never liked it. It reminds me that you think I'm foolish." She paused, then said the rest. "Immature."

"That isn't true, though."

"Then why do you call me that name?" What she really wanted to say was, out of all the nicknames he could have imagined for her, why that one? Did he really only think of her as a harebrained, stupid girl?

He chuckled. "I started thinking of you as 'Silly' when I was dating your sister. You always used to make me smile. I never meant it in a bad way. I promise."

She inwardly winced. "Only that I did stupid things."

"*Nee*. Because you were a bright light next to Beth." Looking as uncomfortable as she was starting to feel, he continued. "Grace, one of the reasons I knew I couldn't continue on with your sister is that she was always looking at the worst of things. She was critical. She found fault with everything."

"Oh." His words were a surprise, and she wasn't even sure what she thought about them.

"I know you might not see that. I know I shouldn't be so honest, but I don't want you thinking that it has anything to do with you, that it wasn't complimentary. I liked a lot of things about Beth, but I knew I wanted to be around someone who lifted me up every day. Not brought me down. Your antics and stories and smile did that."

She stared at him. Wondered how to respond. Wondered if she even should. "I overreacted, John." Hoping to make a joke, she said, "You can call me whatever you like."

He looked at her and shook his head. Then began smiling broadly again. "That's why you're you, Grace King. You never fail to make me see the better side of things."

Against her will, she felt her heart jump at his words. But how could she not? There seemed to be something perfect in between them—and it had been there no matter how much they tried to imagine otherwise.

"Would you like to stay for supper? I was actually making beef enchiladas. I had thought you might want something filling since you've been working hard. Those are ruined now, but I could make something else."

When he said nothing, just stared at her, she swallowed hard. "Or maybe not."

"I had planned to stay, but now I'm thinking that it might be better if I leave."

She felt her skin turn beet red. She'd done it. She'd scared him off. "I understand."

Maybe they did need some time to figure out what had just happened.

He looked at her intently. "I really came over to check on you. How are you feeling? Have you seen anymore footprints? Do you feel safe?"

Did she? Her heart sure didn't. She felt as if it had been torn open and it lay before him, bruised and marred and vulnerable. But ironically, the rest of her did feel safe. Today, after visiting Dorma and now this kitchen fire, she hadn't thought about the mysterious intruder at all.

"Nothing out of the ordinary has happened, John Michael. You don't need to worry about me."

"I'm going to go, then," he murmured, edging closer toward the entryway. "We fought a fire last night and I think I'm still recovering."

Thinking about him being hurt made all of her injured feelings seem "silly" after all. "Wait! Are you all right? Did you get hurt?"

"I did what I needed to do, what I've been trained to do. So yes, I'm perfectly fine." Looking as if he was intent on keeping his emotions at bay, he pulled back on his coat and gloves. "I'll be back tomorrow to check on you."

"There is no need. I can take care of myself."

"Actually, I'm beginning to think that there's every need."

Those words rang in her head as she followed him to the door. As she told him good-bye.

As she stood at the window and watched him leave.

They continued to ring until two tiny paws tapped against her calf. Pleased that Snooze had finally made the first move, Grace bent down and carefully cradled him in her arms. "You are a *gut hund,* Snooze," she murmured into his neck as she cuddled him closer. "A *gut hund,* indeed."

She carried him over to a big easy chair and sat down with him in her arms. Snooze curled on her lap and closed his eyes when she began to pet him.

For the first time all day, she smiled without the slightest reservation. It looked like the day wasn't a disaster after all. At long last, she and Snooze had become friends.

She closed her eyes and gave thanks for rewards in small packages.

# CHAPTER 16

"I'd like you to pay a home visit with me today," Captain Butler said from the doorway of John Michael's bunk room.

His muscles protested when he sat up, but he was pleased he didn't delay too long. "All right. Do you need me to bring anything specific?"

"Just yourself, and your knowledge of Pennsylvania Dutch," he said with a small smile.

"I'll be right there, sir."

"Twenty minutes is soon enough, Rookie."

When he was alone again, John Michael got to his feet. They'd spent the morning practicing cutting people out of cars. Then they went out on a three-mile run. Cleaning the bays had followed that.

By the time he had lunch, every bit of him was exhausted and he was ready for a break. Carter and two of the EMTs were watching television. Though John Michael sometimes sat with them, he'd been yearning for some peace and quiet. He went to his bunk and stretched out, happy to spend an hour reading a British mystery he'd picked up at the library.

After he washed up, he wondered who in the Amish community they were going to visit. He didn't know every Amish person in their area, of course, but he knew a lot of them.

Visiting the Amish in this capacity gave him a feeling of satisfaction. He knew some members of the Amish community didn't trust either the police or other men in uniform. John Michael liked to think he served as a needed bridge between the Amish community and the larger English one.

After straightening his bed and putting the book in his locker, he slipped on the fleece firehouse jacket that they all wore in the winter. It had both his name and the department's name and emblem on it. When he'd gotten it, he'd felt both official and proud.

Now he wondered how his uniform would be received by the Amish man or woman. Some were pleased to have someone in the department speak Pennsylvania Dutch to them, others had a deep distrust of anyone of their background adopting such a mainstream occupation.

Perhaps it didn't matter how they reacted anyway. He'd begun to realize that he couldn't control how people viewed him. All he could control was the way he lived his life.

An hour later, sitting in the passenger seat of the captain's red department-issued SUV, John Michael eyed Dorma Schultz's house with a deep feeling of sadness.

"Her name is Dorma Schultz," Captain Butler said, reading the note in his hand. "Do you know her?"

"I do. My parents bought a part of our farm from her. Her family has been around here for quite some time."

"What did you know of her?"

John Michael shrugged. "She's a widow. She used to go out in the community a lot. Not so much anymore." Though it made him uncomfortable, he forced himself to continue. "I happened to see her at Bill's Diner a couple of days ago. She looked far different. Kind of bedraggled. Nothing like her old self. I'm ashamed to say that, though I haven't seen her in some time, it didn't occur to me to wonder why. I wish I would have thought to stop by. I meant to do that."

Still looking at the paper in his hand, the captain said, "We got a call to do a check on her. Some of her neighbors have been complaining about the state of her yard and home. I think she's been showing some signs of absentmindedness, too."

"I understand."

"Grab a pack of batteries and a smoke detector. We'll go inside to check that, make sure it's in good shape. Then we'll go from there."

"Sounds good." After getting the two items, he walked to the captain's side and knocked on the door.

When they didn't hear any response, he knocked again. "Miss Schultz?" he called out. "Miss Schultz, it's John Michael Miller," he said in Pennsylvania Dutch.

Then they heard some footsteps and saw the fluttering of the lace curtain to the side of the door. John smiled, hoping he looked at least a little familiar to her.

At last the door opened.

"Yes?" Miss Schultz was dressed in a faded gray dress that had obviously once been made to fit a larger frame. The straight pins that held its front together, where there was quite a bit of extra material, were crooked. The gray hair under her *kapp* looked thin and tangled. He wondered when she'd last bathed and changed clothes.

"Miss Schultz, do you remember me?" he asked slowly. "I'm John Michael. You used to bring me candy when you came over to visit."

She peered at him closer. *"Nee."*

He tried again. "My parents bought some of your land for our farm. We used to bring you corn every year. One time I stayed to husk it with you."

"You lost a *zaah*," she murmured when her eyes cleared.

Remembering the day she was speaking of, he nodded. *"Jah,* that is right. I lost a tooth, one of my front ones." Smiling softly, he added, "You promised me that it would grow back one day."

She smiled suddenly, looking like the woman she'd once been. "And so it did."

Feeling like they'd at last established a connection, he gestured to Captain Butler. "This is Zack. He's my boss. We came to check to make sure you have a smoke detector that works."

Captain Butler held up the brand-new smoke detector in his hand. "Do you have one of these, Miss Schultz?"

She stared at him, appearing very flustered. "I don't know."

"How about I look around and you have a cup of tea with John Michael, here, while I install this?" Captain Butler asked.

John was taken aback. "Sir, I can do that."

"No, what you are doing is more important." He made a motion with his hand. "Go on, now."

John Michael gestured toward the kitchen. "Would you like some tea, Dorma?"

She nodded and led the way.

To his surprise, the room was far cleaner than either the living room or the entryway. The sink only had two glasses in it, the counters were shiny, and the floor was swept. After he found the mugs and located the kettle, which also looked freshly scrubbed, he smiled at her. "Have you been busy cleaning or did someone come in to help?"

"Grace came."

"Oh? Is that right?" he asked as he located the tea bags. "God's grace is *gut*, for sure."

"*Nee. Grace* came. She helped me." Pointing to a box filled with scones and waxed paper, she added, "She brought me cinnamon cookies."

He recognized those scones. John felt his throat tighten as he realized that Grace had come over on her own and had taken the initiative to help in Miss Schultz's kitchen. She really was a woman to be proud of.

"Grace is a nice lady," he said as he sat down beside her. "I bet her cookies are *gut*. Who else has come to see you lately?"

And just like that, her expression became blank again. "I don't know," she blurted, looking worried. "I don't know."

"That's all right, then," he murmured. "You don't have to know. But I am going to make sure that I come over again soon."

Captain Butler joined them in the kitchen. "I found an old one in the bedroom." Looking a little pained, he added, "I switched it out and tested it, but we should probably remind her about what it does."

"*Jah.* Of course." Taking her hand, he walked Dorma to her bedroom. It was a mess of discarded clothes, trash, discarded books, and mail. Off to the side was an uncomfortable-looking twin-sized bed. The sheets were rumpled. Making a mental note to speak to his mother so she could come over and help Dorma with her clothes, he pointed to the ceiling. "This is your new smoke detector." He was tall enough to press a button so that he could sound the test.

It let out a piercing beep.

Dorma put her hands over her ears. "*Halt!*"

"That noise is going to go off if you have a fire," Captain Butler said clearly and distinctly. "If you hear that, you need to leave your house right away. Do you understand?"

John Michael repeated the words in Pennsylvania Dutch, ending with "This is important. You must try to remember."

She nodded. "I will remember."

"I'll be back soon," John Michael said as they walked back into her living room.

Dorma stopped and stared at him intently. "You really will?"

He nodded. "I really will. I promise."

She didn't walk them out. Instead, she sat on a rocking chair and stared at the ceiling.

"That woman can't live by herself any longer," the captain said. "Do you have any contacts in your community so we can find out where her next of kin is? Or someone who could help?"

"I'll do that. A friend of mine stopped by, but you're right. She needs more help than an occasional visitor. It isn't enough."

"She shouldn't be using her stove or oven. It's not safe."

"I agree." He promised himself that he would make things right as soon as he could.

He hoped he would be able to make good on that vow.

# CHAPTER 17

After taking Snooze out for a short walk, Grace turned on the Lees' Christmas tree lights. It was a ten-foot-tall blue spruce and decorated with at least a thousand white lights. Mrs. Lee had festooned it with all sorts of ornaments. Some were handmade, others looked like they were made of crystal and had the dates carefully engraved on the center of each. Grace thought they were very beautiful. However, what had caught her eye from the first were the gaily decorated animals. There were all sorts of animals: white cows with wreaths around their necks, camels holding jeweled boxes, elephants adorned with satin ribbons.

There were also dozens and dozens of jeweled dog bones.

Grace had laughed when she'd realized what the glittering ornaments actually were. Milk-Bone dog biscuits had been carefully covered in shiny paint and painstakingly decorated with beads, rhinestones, and sequins. Right away, she'd fallen in love with the sight.

She felt a little guilty about it, too, because those decorated bones were just the type of thing her sometimes-stern father would say was wrong with the Englishers' Christmas traditions. Daed liked to believe that the Englishers placed too much emphasis on the shiny and loud and not enough on what really mattered, which was the miracle of Jesus's birth.

As for herself, Grace wasn't sure if the Lees were ignoring the real reason for the season or simply were whimsical by nature. She supposed it didn't matter to her. They had been nice when they'd hired her to watch Snooze. And Snooze, for all of his own silly character traits, seemed like he was happy with his situation.

It wasn't for her to judge if they were celebrating Christmas the "right" way or not.

A momentary pang of loneliness crept through her. She wondered what her family was doing, then realized she knew exactly what her mother and sisters would be up to so close to Christmas. Beth, Leona, and Sylvia would be shopping and baking and planning and visiting with extended relatives. Her brothers Johnny and Dan would probably be sleeping as much as possible, enjoying a short break from the farm.

No doubt they were all also staying up late and sharing the same stories they always did. Maybe eating pumpkin pie at midnight. And helping to take care of her grandparents, of course.

Grace needed to remember that. There was a reason they had left, and it was because they were needed. Someone else's needs were far greater than her own. She really should be less selfish.

She'd just pulled out a sheet of paper, planning to write them a quick note, when the phone rang. It was only the second or third time hearing it ring since she'd been there.

"Hello?" she asked tentatively, thinking it must be Mr. or Mrs. Lee.

"Grace?"

"Mamm?" She sat down on the big easy chair next to the tree. "I was just thinking about you. How are you? How are Mommi and Dawdi?"

"They are finally doing better, praise *Got.*"

"I am glad." Her bottom lip quivered. Ironically, now her ache for them grew stronger. "Please tell them I hope they'll continue to feel better soon."

"I will do that. But Grace, I called because all of us have been worried about you. How are you? What have you been doing?"

"Me? Oh, I am fine. Don't worry about me none."

"That's no answer. Tell me what you've been doing. Is that *hund* behaving himself?"

She smiled. Her mother always sounded as if every dog was actually a wild animal. "Snooze is fine. Though at first, he gave me quite a scare. He chased a squirrel into the woods next to the Lees' *haus*. I was so afraid I had lost him or he was stuck in the snow."

"Did you find him all right? Were you warm enough?"

Even from so far away, her mother was trying to mother her! "I was all right." Then she realized where this conversational tangent had brought her—right to John Michael Miller's side. Did she dare bring up his name?

But how could she not when he had done so much for her?

"Mamm, actually Snooze introduced me to an old friend."

"Oh? Who was that?"

"Actually, it was John Michael."

Her voice hardened. "John Michael Miller?"

"*Jah.*" Uh-oh. Bringing up his name was obviously a bad idea. "It turns out that his farm lies right next to the Lees' house. He helped me look through the snow for Snooze." And he'd given her the very coat off his back so she wouldn't get chilled. And walked her back so that she would get home safely.

She forced a laugh, even though she feared it sounded beyond fake and brittle. "Talk about a small world."

"I hope you reminded him that he broke your sister's heart."

"We talked about Beth. He knows he hurt her."

"Well, I hope you won't have to see him again. Then we won't ever have to tell your sister that you talked to him."

Even though it probably wasn't the right time, Grace knew she couldn't do that. "He explained his side of the story, Mamm. Now isn't the right time to discuss it all, but I don't believe he knowingly meant to do her harm."

"It doesn't matter if he meant to do harm or not, child. He did."

She closed her eyes, then moved forward. "Mamm, I've seen him quite a few times since."

"You have done what?"

Grace winced. "He's come by to check on me and Snooze. He even helped me when a pan on the stove caught fire. He's a fire-fighter now, you see."

"It isn't like you to be so careless. Or so thoughtless of your sister's feelings."

"I had an accident. Everyone has them," she said, echoing his earlier words. "And I haven't been insensitive. I'm trying to tell you that I don't think that he's as unkind as we had originally thought."

She heard her mother sigh on the phone. "I think I know what is really at the root of all of this."

"And what is that?"

"You have always coveted him. Even when Beth was in love, you had a crush on John Michael Miller."

That stung. Both because her mother was refusing to listen to her but also because it was true. Her cheeks heated with shame. "Mother, I haven't talked to you in days. Must we discuss this now?"

"If you're avoiding talking about him, I think we know why."

Grace stood up and began to pace. "If I am wanting to avoid talking about John Michael, it is because you aren't wanting to listen to anything I have to say. He has been a good friend to me. Now, may we please talk about something else?"

"Such as what? How your sister is going to be heartbroken when she finds out what you've been doing?"

"Why is it always about Beth and her broken heart?" Before she could stop herself, she blurted, "You know what? I was really afraid the other day. I found footprints near the house and I had feared someone had broken in. I was so afraid, I picked up Snooze and ran all the way to the Millers' *haus*. John Michael stopped everything when he saw me and called the sheriff. He even came over and stayed with me while the sheriff was here."

"What? Were you harmed? And the sheriff? Oh, Grace. This job of yours . . ."

And there it came again. The slight criticism. And maybe it was justified, but it made her feel even more frustrated. "All I'm trying to tell you is that things here have not been easy and I've missed you all. I didn't want to be away from you. I'm only trying to do the right thing. I had promised the Lees that I'd stay with Snooze months ago. I couldn't go back on that."

After a pause, her mother sighed. "You are right. Are . . . are you all right now?"

"*Jah.* I think so."

"*Gut.* You know . . . oh! Hold on." Grace could hear her say something to someone standing nearby. "I'm sorry but one of your grandparents' neighbors wants to use the phone so I'm going to go. Daed or I will call again soon. Bye now."

"Bye, Mamm. *Ich leevi dich.*"

"I love you too, Grace. Good day."

When the phone clicked and the room went silent, Grace sat back down and tried to wrap her head around the fact that no matter what she told John Michael, it seemed as if her heart had already made up its mind. The feelings she'd had for him all those years ago were back, and alive and well.

And now her whole family was going to know it, too.

# CHAPTER 18

Grace was still reeling from the phone call with her mother when John Michael knocked on the door two hours later.

"Hiya," he said, looking awkward. "How are you feeling today?"

There was surely no way she was going to tell him about her recent phone call. "All right." Attempting to smile, she said, "I haven't had another kitchen accident, so that's something to celebrate."

"Indeed." He smiled, but the humor didn't quite reach his eyes.

And just like that, some of the hurt feelings she'd been holding tight fell away. "John Michael, you don't look too good. Is something wrong?"

"*Nee.* Well, maybe." He shrugged. "To be honest, I'm not exactly sure."

"It sounds like you need to talk about it." Glad to focus on his problems instead of her own, she said, "Take off your coat and come sit down."

After shrugging off his coat and hanging it on the knob, he faced her. "I paid a visit to Dorma Schultz yesterday. She told me that you had called on her, too." Looking almost tentative, he said, "Could I speak to you about her? I'm worried."

"I've been worried about Dorma, too. Would you like some cookies or something?"

His expression warmed. "Did you bake again?"

"I canna help it, I guess. Would you like one? They're eggnog cookies."

He wrinkled his nose. "*Danke,* but not right now. I just really needed to talk to you."

"Let's go sit by the Christmas tree."

As John Michael followed her toward the living room, he looked around the space like he had before. Then, when they got to the room, he paused in front of the Christmas tree. It was ablaze with beautiful white lights. And because the day had been overcast, it seemed even brighter than usual.

He gazed at it in obvious appreciation. "This is a beautiful sight, isn't it?"

She nodded. "Don't tell anyone, but I sometimes wish that we could have a Christmas tree in our home." Fingering one of the silly bejeweled dog bones, she smiled. "Without the bones, though."

He chuckled and pointed to one of the animal ornaments. It was a prancing fox, complete with a top hat and purple coat. "Or the dressed-up creatures."

She sat down. "Why were you over at Dorma's house?"

"My captain asked if I would go over there with him since she's Amish. From time to time we do care visits like that. Checking on residents someone has reported a concern about."

"I have no doubt that someone has called about her. She was pretty confused when I saw her."

"I found the same thing to be true. The captain installed a new smoke alarm in her bedroom. We explained to her that if it sounded, she needed to get out right away." He paused. "To be honest, I'm not sure if I stopped by there today she would remember me."

"I'm really worried about her. What do you think we should do?"

His expression warmed again, making her feel like he was proud of her, but for what, she couldn't imagine. "She might not remember me, but I think you made an impression on her. She brought up your name." As if he was thinking of a private joke, he said, "When she first mentioned 'Grace,' I thought she was speaking of God's grace. It was only after she revealed that you'd brought her cinnamon cookies and I noticed that they were these scones that I put two and two together."

"I enjoyed talking with her, but I can't say I felt too good about my visit when I left. I felt the same way you did."

"Captain Butler is going to talk to Sheriff Brewer. Someone over at the sheriff's department is going to do some searching to see if she has any family in the area. But I thought maybe, in the meantime, the two of us could look in on her as often as possible, at least through Christmas."

"I'd be happy to do that. Thank you for asking me to help out," said Grace.

"Only you would say asking to look on an elderly person in need of care was doing you a favor."

"Maybe not. I'd like to think that most people are simply waiting to be asked to do something for somebody else."

"I've never thought of it that way, but you might be right." He looked as if he wanted to say something more, but paused. "You seem quiet. Are you upset about how we left things off the other day?"

After debating for a moment, Grace decided to share what was weighing on her so deeply. "Maybe, but it has more to do with a phone call I received earlier today. It was my mother."

Concern etched his features. "Have your grandparents' health gotten worse?"

"I don't believe so. It had to do with something else." Musing, she continued, "I love my family and I love being with them. I miss them, too. But I recently came to the conclusion that everything about me is not tied up into them."

"I don't understand."

"I'm not surprised. I am still trying to come to terms with it. But, well, what I'm trying to say is that I guess I've realized that it's possible for me to make decisions that don't have anything to do with my parents' wishes. Or even my sisters' wishes or advice. I've become my own person."

He nodded slowly. "That happened to me a few years back. It . . . well, it was a revelation."

She loved that he wasn't making light of her statement. Appreciated that John Michael was feeling some of the very same things that she was. It made her feel not so alone.

It also brought forth a question. "What did you do after you realized that?"

"What do you mean?"

"Did it change you? Or, did it change the way you related to the rest of your family?"

He paused. "You know . . . *nee*."

"Really?" She wasn't sure if that made her feel better or if it was disappointing. Part of her felt like such a monumental change in her life should have repercussions in every other part of her life, too.

He shrugged. "I'm no expert, Grace. All I know is how I reacted. And, to be honest, I never spent a lot of time considering how my realization would affect the rest of my life. But . . . if I had to say, I think it made me more patient with my parents."

"More patient?" That was a surprise.

"I felt more settled inside, you know? I kind of felt like I wasn't relying on someone else to tell me how I should act or feel. I wasn't looking for approval anymore. I had found a new sense of peace within myself."

Grace realized that his words made a lot of sense, and that this new change of heart wasn't going to be easy . . . but that maybe it wasn't going to be so hard, either. "I'm glad I told you what I was feeling."

"Are you? I don't feel like I helped."

Lifting her chin slightly, she smiled. "My new, improved self would say that I didn't necessarily tell you so that you would help me. I told you because you asked."

The smile that had been playing on his lips grew. "Whew! I can tell that this new Grace is gonna be a force to be reckoned with."

She chuckled. "Don't forget. You've been forewarned."

"Would you like to bundle up and go for a walk? Maybe make plans to visit Miss Schultz soon?"

"I would. It's cold out but not terrible. It will be nice to get outside for a while."

While she went to gather her mittens and a scarf, he walked over to unplug the cord behind the tree. When several needles rained down on the carpet, he frowned. "When was the last time you watered the tree, Grace?"

"The tree was cut down, *silly*. I haven't watered it."

He didn't laugh at her comment. Instead, he knelt down and pointed to the metal container that the tree was fastened into. "Do you see this, Grace? You're supposed to keep it filled with water so the trunk can absorb it. The water will keep the needles from falling and lessen the chance of fire."

Getting up, he crossed to the kitchen. "Help me look for a water pitcher. We'll go take care of it now."

After opening a couple of cabinets, she located a plastic pitcher and filled it about halfway with water. John Michael took it from her and crouched by the tree to fill the container. "Don't forget to check this every day."

"I won't."

She took the pitcher from him and felt some of the lightness she'd been feeling between them dissipate.

Thinking about how he always seemed to want to take care of her instead of be with her, she said, "I'm really not as scatterbrained as you seem to think I am."

"I don't think of you as scatterbrained at all."

"Are you sure?" Thinking of all the warnings he'd given her, she said, "I feel like you don't think I can do anything right."

"That's not true." He walked closer to her. Close enough that she could spy the sincerity in his expression. "All I'm trying to do is keep you safe, Grace. I . . ." He swallowed. "Well, I would be devastated if something happened to you. I don't know if I could bear it."

Suddenly, all of her worries about him thinking of her as child-ish and immature faded. She saw the same concern for her that she felt for him reflected in his expression. "I feel the same way about you when you go to work," she admitted.

He reached out and quietly ran a finger down her cheek. The light touch should have been barely noticeable, but she felt it down to her toes. "I guess we'll have to do our best to keep each other safe, then, Grace."

Before she could reply, he strode toward the door.

Leaving her to pick up Snooze and follow.

# CHAPTER 19

"Hope you ate your Wheaties last night, Miller," Captain Butler said as they entered the firehouse together at seven o'clock the next morning.

"I don't know what that means," John Michael said. "I'm thinking it has something to do with you working us hard today?" He could only imagine the training exercises the captain had up his sleeve.

"Yep. You're on the right track. But it's not me that's going to be working us hard. It's the season. Yesterday's crew got called out for two vehicular accidents and one kitchen fire."

Though he knew Captain Butler expected a lighthearted response, John Michael couldn't summon a joke. "I'll be prepared to do my best."

After a beat, the captain clapped him on the back. "You're right, rookie. The best is all we can do."

As always, the first thing they did after putting their personal items in the lockers was start a load of laundry since the last thing each member of the previous crew did before leaving was strip their sheets. It was then up to the next team to wash the sheets and make their beds.

And because John Michael was the most junior member of his team, the bulk of the laundry duty usually fell on his shoulders. It was something that never failed to strike him as funny. He'd grown up thinking that doing laundry was strictly women's work.

But he quickly learned that carrying around linens and towels from four men and four beds wasn't all that light. Thinking of how his *mamm* had always washed the clothes in the basement of their home before carrying it upstairs to the clothesline outside, he felt ashamed. He should have never taken that for granted. Or, at the very least, he should have offered to carry up the wicker basket of wet laundry for her.

He had only time to start the first load of laundry when their captain called them together. Sitting around the kitchen table, he listened intently as Captain Butler read notes from the company log.

It described the vehicular accidents and the kitchen fire in greater detail, as well as the number of community and home visits the team had gone on.

Looking up from his notes, Captain Butler turned to him. "In regards to Dorma Schultz, Deputy Beck said he was going to put her on his rotation. So far, he hasn't been able to get ahold of any of her next of kin."

"I spoke with a friend of mine who is going to join me on paying Miss Dorma visits, too," John Michael said. "She'll be looked after."

"Glad to hear that." After assigning jobs for the morning, the captain pulled out his phone. "So, I wanted to give you an update on the suspicious fires," he began, his voice turning more serious. "I received a memo late last night from the fire inspector and Sheriff Brewer." He sighed. "The news is, there is no news. No other county in the state is experiencing an outbreak of this sort. And, beyond the usual holiday spike in robberies, the sheriff doesn't have anything conclusive to report."

Hank crossed his arms over his chest. "That's it?"

John Michael thought Hank's incredulous tone spoke for all of them. There had to be some way to stop the trend.

"Unfortunately, yes. The sheriff's department is going to try to up their patrols, but y'all know as well as I do that's going to be hard to do. This is a busy time for all of us, what with the weather and the increase in vehicular accidents."

Pausing for a moment, he shoved his phone in the pocket of his jacket. "Is there anything else that we need to discuss? Anyone have anything to add?"

"Nothing besides that I heard it was supposed to start sleeting this afternoon," Sean said.

"I'll put extra blankets in each truck," Hank said, then grinned, breaking the tension in the room. "And remind everyone that it's Anderson's turn to cook tonight."

"Best news I've heard all week," the captain said, looking pleased. John Michael knew why, too. Anderson was the best cook in their firehouse.

"What are you making?" he asked.

"Chicken Kiev, rice, and steamed vegetables."

Hank grunted. "Sounds kind of healthy."

"It is," Anderson replied. "We're firefighters, idiot."

While the other men chuckled, the captain shook his head in mock annoyance. "Now that our dinner plans are taken care of, it's time to get to work. Check your inventories, check your equipment, and help wash down the garage. It's going to be a busy day."

He wasn't wrong. Before an hour had passed, the bells were ringing and John Michael was putting on his turnout gear.

"Miller, go with the pumper truck," the captain ordered. "We've got a fire that erupted during another robbery."

His SCBA already on, John Michael jumped in the passenger seat of the pumper as it pulled out, following the flashing lights and sirens of the ladder truck down the street.

FOURTEEN HOURS LATER, he was lounging in one of the recliners in the dayroom and nursing a couple of burns and a nasty cut on his left arm. He'd gotten both from their last call—an elderly couple's home on the outskirts of town. The space heater they'd been using had faulty wiring and had sparked a fire.

That spark—combined with the couple's panic and the fact that it looked as if they hadn't thrown anything out in the last thirty years—had created a good-sized blaze by the time their team had arrived on the scene.

Praise God that the couple had survived, though all of them had gotten a scare when they saw just how close the couple was standing to the fire.

Captain Butler had eventually learned that while the couple got right out to safety, their cat wasn't as eager to run through the smoke. Presumably, it had hid. Both the husband and wife were standing at the doorway of their burning house and calling for it.

And that sight had John Michael both shaking his head in frustration and in pity. Of course no one wanted to see a pet perish in a fire, but the couple very nearly lost their lives being so close to the burning timbers.

Barely five minutes after he and Hank pulled the couple away, the porch came tumbling down. If the man and woman had still been standing there, they would've been crushed by the debris.

After they were guided to safety, John manned the pumper truck, monitoring it and keeping in contact with the chief in case they needed to call for another unit.

Luckily, it wasn't needed. Within the next half-hour, the flames were extinguished and the couple was taken away in an ambulance.

Only when the team returned to the firehouse and started cleaning up had John realized he sustained a couple of minor injuries. Sean spied the cuts and carefully treated them.

Captain Butler had even questioned him, wanting to make sure that John hadn't made a mistake in protocol or safety.

Now, after eating a helping of Anderson's chicken Kiev, followed by some chicken-and-rice casserole that volunteers had kindly brought by, all of them were trying to rest up.

"As bad as this makes me sound, I kind of hate December," Sean said. "We get so many calls like that last one. People using faulty heaters."

"That doesn't happen just in December," the captain murmured, his eyes on the muted basketball game playing on the television. "Y'all know we're going to get these calls for the next three months."

"I know. But it just seems worse when there's Christmas lights up."

"Can't fault you there," Hank said. "At least we haven't had a Christmas tree fire today. I hate when we see the kids crying and saying that Santa isn't going to know where to find them."

Sean glanced John Michael's way. "What do you hate about this season?"

John tried to come up with something that would make him sound like he was one of the gang, but he didn't want to lie. "Not any of that," he replied, feeling that he was about to sound a bit too positive or hopeful. "I guess I canna help but feel grateful that we're here. If not for us, all those people could be even worse off."

Sean sat up. "Really?" he asked incredulously. "That's all you can say?"

John Michael felt his cheeks flush, but he didn't back down. "My family used to live even farther out in the country. One day some brush my father was burning got out of hand. We lost a horse."

He took a deep breath, attempting to remove the memory of that awful day. "We didn't have a phone, of course. And we lived so far out that it took awhile for anyone who did have a phone to call about it."

"Wow. I never knew you went through that," the captain said. "That must have been terrible."

"It was. Losing that poor horse, *and* the barn, then worrying that we were going to lose our *haus*—and seeing my parents able to do nothing but stand hopelessly by as we hoped and prayed for help?—that was a difficult day, for sure." Clearing his throat to push away the sudden lump that had formed there, he continued quietly. "I canna help but be grateful that we're here helping people."

"Good point." The captain clapped him on the shoulder. "Okay, men, I'm going to try to get some rest. I suggest you do the same. I'd be real surprised if we don't get another call before dawn."

Sean stood up. "I'll hit the sack, too."

John Michael felt his eyes get heavy, though he wasn't sure if he would be able to rest or not. Now that he'd brought back up those memories, he knew all that would happen if he tried to lie down and sleep were nightmares of that fateful day.

He decided to sit there a little longer. He never minded the silence and he could simply stare blindly at the game.

Anderson stood up when another set of commercials came on. "Hey, John Michael?"

"*Jah?*" he asked, realizing how far his mind had drifted since he'd forgotten to speak English.

Sean stuffed his hands in his pockets. "What you said earlier . . . well, I'm just glad you did. Thanks."

Though John Michael was about to say it wasn't anything, he elected to simply nod instead. He'd felt as if the Lord had given him those words.

As if God had known that he needed to remember his value.

Five minutes later, still in his chair, he fell asleep.

And four hours later, he was startled awake by the bells chiming . . . and was rushing downstairs yet again.

# CHAPTER 20

Grace had meant to leave Dorma's house an hour ago, but there was so much to do she kept pushing back her departure. She'd made Dorma a chicken-and-broccoli casserole and some pumpkin scones. She'd also changed her sheets and did a load of laundry. For once, she was thankful that it was winter, with a clothesline for laundry in the basement. She could hang the sheets and towels there. And even if Dorma didn't remember to go downstairs until Grace returned, the linens would dry and not be forgotten outside.

Now they were sitting at Dorma's freshly polished kitchen table and putting together a simple jigsaw puzzle that she'd brought with her.

It had a cute Christmas scene. A snowman, lots of green trees, snow, blue sky, and some brown hares. It was a rather easy one—only a hundred pieces. At first, Grace was worried that even this was too much for Dorma.

But after a shaky start, she seemed to enjoy the activity. Once she got another pair of pieces together, she looked up at Grace with a pleased smile. "Another match!"

"*Gut* for you!" Grace said. "Before you know it, we'll have half of it done."

"Do you really think so?"

"Yes," she said encouragingly. "But even if we don't get much further today, it's okay. *I'm* having fun working on it."

"It *is* fun." As Dorma moved some pieces around again, a small frown appeared in the middle of her forehead. "I don't remember the last time I did a puzzle. I used to enjoy them."

"We can work on them as often as you'd like. I'll bring another one over in a few days."

Dorma set the two pieces she was manipulating down on the table. "You'll come back again?" She seemed confused.

"Of course I will. I promised I would." When Dorma still looked doubtful, Grace said, "I enjoy being with you." Then Grace smiled. It occurred to her that she wasn't exaggerating. Visiting Dorma had brightened her day. She'd been so depressed and upset about the conversation with her mother, and she didn't know how to come to terms with it—well, besides knowing that she was right and her mother was wrong.

"I like being with you, too, Grace," Dorma said.

She'd remembered her name! Swallowing back a wave of emotion, Grace picked up another couple of pieces. "Let's try and get a few more of these pesky pieces together before it's time for me to leave and for you to take a break."

Following her lead, Dorma rearranged her glasses, then turned to Grace in alarm when her doorbell rang.

"It's all right. I'll get it," she soothed. "You stay here and keep working." Quickly walking to the door, she peeked through the little hole in the door . . . then smiled broadly. "John Michael is here!"

Dorma frowned. "I don't know John Michael."

"I think you might remember him when you see his face," she murmured as she opened the door. And stood there smiling. "Hi."

"Hi, back," he said. "This is a nice surprise."

"I guess great minds think alike."

"I guess so." He walked in, looked like he wanted to add something more private, but he strode over to see Dorma first. "Hi, Miss Schultz. Do you remember that I said I was going to come by again real soon?"

Looking tense and agitated, she shook her head.

"That's okay if you don't remember," he said patiently. "I remember you. I'm going to take off my coat and stay for a while. Okay?"

Dorma stared at him for a long moment before turning back to Grace.

"He's a friend," Grace said.

Dorma frowned before slowly returning her attention back to the puzzle, but it was obvious that John Michael's arrival had set her off. She seemed more agitated and ill at ease.

Hoping to soften the moment, Grace picked up her mug. "We've been drinking cinnamon tea," she informed him. "Would you like some?"

*"Nee. Danke."*

She laughed at his expression. "You're not a fan of flavored teas?"

"I don't know if I am or not. Only that I know I don't want to try cinnamon tea." He made a face. "I'll get some water instead."

"I can help you get it."

*"Nee.* You sit down. I didn't come over here to be waited on." After he got himself a glass of water, he joined them at the square table. "Dorma, last time I was here, I told you that the deputy and I were going to do a little bit of searching for your relatives. We located one of your nieces, Martha. Does that ring a bell?"

Her eyes lit up. "Martha likes spaghetti."

John Michael smiled. "That may be true, but she likes you, too. Unfortunately, she lives in Michigan now. That's pretty far away. She did mention that you have some other relatives who live closer." He pulled out a small notebook. "A Benjamin and a Samuel. Do you—"

*"Nee!"*

"What?"

"I don't like them." She got to her feet and started moving backward, stopping only when her back got to the wall. "They canna come here."

Alarmed, Grace ran to her side. "John, she's trembling."

He stepped forward, then froze. It was obvious that John Michael didn't know how to make things better instead of worse. After a moment, he held up his hands in surrender. "They won't come here. They're not anywhere close," he continued slowly. "I'm sorry I brought up their names."

But John Michael's efforts were in vain. Instead of looking comforted, Dorma closed her eyes and hugged herself tightly. "*Nee, nee, nee,*" she whispered.

Becoming even more alarmed, Grace met John's gaze. "What now?" she mouthed.

"I don't know," he whispered back. "But I don't think she can live here much longer by herself."

Nodding back at him, Grace feared he was right.

Slowly approaching Dorma, Grace softened her voice as much as she could. "You need to rest. I made your bed, remember? Let me help you get settled."

Opening her eyes, Dorma stared at her before finally nodding.

"I'll be right back," Grace whispered to John Michael as she wrapped a comforting arm around Dorma's shoulders and escorted her to her bedroom.

Luckily, Dorma seemed ready to lie down and didn't protest when Grace helped her take off her shoes and get settled. "You found my keepsake box," she murmured.

"I did. It's so pretty, Dorma."

Grace had discovered the rather large wooden box when she was changing the bed's sheets. It was made of cherrywood and surprisingly heavy. When she'd peeked inside and noticed that it was filled with letters, Grace decided to place it on Dorma's bedside table.

"I have a special box for my favorite things, too," she murmured, but realized that the older lady had already fallen fast asleep.

When she returned to the kitchen area, Grace noticed that John had already cleared the table of their mugs, neatly washed everything, and set them on the countertop.

"Is she all right?" he asked.

"I think so. She's already fast asleep."

"That's good. No doubt she needs her rest."

Thinking about Dorma's panic attack and the neglected house—and her fragile state of mind—she stared at John Michael. "What are we going to do? She mustn't stay here much longer by herself."

"I fear you are right. If we don't do something soon, she's going to hurt herself." Reaching for her hand, he squeezed it gently. "Try not to worry. Several people are looking for her relatives. Someone will turn up."

Grace nodded, but she had a bad feeling about Dorma's future. Someone had to help this woman who used to help them so many years ago.

She just hoped John Michael could find that person very soon.

# CHAPTER 21

"Tell me about Benjamin and Samuel," Grace said as they walked back to the Lees' house. Bundled up in her black cloak and bonnet, wearing her red mittens and scarf, she strolled side-by-side with John on the black asphalt road, a majority of which was now snow-free.

John Michael braced himself. He wasn't surprised that she brought up the two men who had put Dorma into such a state, but he wished he had better news to share with her.

"They're Dorma's younger *bruder*'s sons. Her nephews. And from what Deputy Beck has been able to discern, they couldn't be more disreputable if they tried."

"It's obvious she can't stay with them, even if they are her own kin. She was afraid just hearing their names."

Sharing her opinion, he nodded. "I completely agree. From what I understand, they're not functioning like themselves. One of them, or maybe both now, has a drug problem. They have police records, too."

"They've been arrested?"

"Yep. And served some jail time for aggravated robbery. From what Deputy Beck pieced together, it looks like they hit Dorma's house two or three years ago."

Her eyes widened, then she seemed to come to terms with what she was hearing. Watching that naiveté slowly fade was hard for him to watch. He hated that this December Grace seemed to be coming face-to-face with more than her fair share of hardships and pain. He stayed silent while she processed it. Though the news was unpleasant, it was also the reality of the situation. If Grace really wanted to help Dorma, then she needed to know the truth.

At last she spoke. "Those nephews . . . are they Amish?"

"They were raised Amish, but they jumped the fence."

"How old are they? Do you know?"

Feeling grim, he replied, "They're young but old enough to know better. Seventeen and eighteen."

"I don't think there's any age where what they're doing is all right." She frowned. "If they were raised in our faith, I don't understand how they came to sink so low."

He shrugged. "I've learned that you can never know what happens in each person's private house, Grace. Maybe something happened there. Or maybe they just ran wild. That happens, too."

"I suppose," she said as they paused at the intersection in the road.

While they crossed, he tried to give her as much information as he could. "Deputy Beck said the brothers left their parents soon after eighth grade. They haven't done much of anything but descend into an awful downward spiral." He cleared his throat. "But I do have a little bit of good news to share."

"What is that?"

"They were recently seen in one of the motels near Mammoth Cave. Deputy Beck is going to try to speak with them, maybe even take them in for questioning."

She looked even more disturbed. "John Michael, we both saw the state that Miss Dorma was in. Why did you even mention those boys? If you knew they were so bad, you should've kept your news to yourself. All it did was upset her."

It wasn't like he hadn't felt badly the minute he witnessed Dorma's reaction. "I didn't mean to bring them up to frighten her. I really was just trying to mention a couple of family names, trying to help her connect again. Obviously, it backfired. But that said, I'm not visiting her only out of compassion. I'm there because I was asked to keep tabs on her. It's part of my job." He hoped she understood.

"What did that niece say? Maybe she can help rein them in."

"Beck spoke to her. But any help from her is a no-go. She and her husband have their hands full with their own lives up in Michigan. And according to Beck, they're a little worried about Dorma—though not enough to actually help her much." He hated to be the bearer of bad news and hated even more to see Grace's reaction to it. Slowly, he continued. "After a little more digging, I learned that some of the relatives feel that she kept money from them after the sale of the family's ranch. They are blaming her for Samuel and Benjamin's problems."

"That doesn't make any sense!"

She looked so affronted, John Michael almost smiled. "Grace, it happens sometimes. Deputy Beck said the niece has convinced herself that if Dorma had given more money to the rest of the family, the boys wouldn't have left home so early and taken this downward path."

Grace stopped in her tracks. "That's awful. It doesn't make a lick of sense, either."

"I agree." He hated how upset she looked. "Hey, try not to worry. The important thing is that we're all going through the proper channels. We can't move Dorma without making sure that there is no one else who can help."

"I don't like how doing the right thing feels so wrong."

"I don't like it either, but we've got to abide by the laws," he said as he moved closer to her when a buggy drove by.

Putting her head down, she nodded. "I understand."

"Hey. This might not help make you feel better, but there is a silver lining."

"What could that be?"

"If we hadn't gone to Bill's, neither of us would've seen Miss Schultz there. All of this would've still been going on, but no one would've been helping her."

She stared at him in surprise. "I had forgotten that all of us were there the same day." She shook her head. "What were the chances?"

"I don't think it was coincidence, Grace."

She shook her head. "I don't believe that, either." Looking more sure of herself, she added, "The Lord really has been looking out for Dorma."

"I think so. Just as He's been looking out for both of us, too."

"He did bring you to me at the perfect time that other day," she said with a smile. "If you hadn't appeared when you did, the Lees' kitchen could've really been damaged."

"Maybe Jesus wasn't as worried about the Lees' kitchen as He was about you."

"You and Jesus have helped me so much."

"See? There you go. I've helped you . . . like you've helped me."

"Hmm, I don't think that's exactly right. Because of you? I'm taken care of. And so is Dorma. For the life of me, I can't imagine how I've helped your life, though. I seem to have only brought you more problems than you know what to do with."

"I wouldn't agree."

"Oh? You can see some benefit?"

As far as he was concerned, everything in his life had gotten better when he'd spied her in the woods. He'd felt hope again. He'd found a purpose again. Some of the bitterness and sense of being out of sync with most everyone and everything had faded. In its place was a new goal—and a deep yearning for her.

Suddenly, he completely understood why he had never felt like Beth was the one for him. He understood why he'd been so uncomfortable about his feelings for Grace.

It wasn't that he shouldn't have fallen in love with Grace, it was that his love for her was so strong, nothing was going to be able to stand in its way.

"I guess maybe you don't," Grace said.

"Hmm?" He'd been so busy realizing that he'd fallen in love, he'd forgotten their conversation.

"I asked if you saw any benefit of the two of us coming to-gether," she said. "By your silence, I'm guessing you haven't found a thing."

He yearned to tell her exactly how he was feeling but he couldn't risk losing her. "*Nee,* Grace. The opposite has been true. I haven't found only one benefit from being in your company. I've discov-ered almost too many benefits to count."

# CHAPTER 22

The call had come at exactly ten in the morning and Grace picked up the phone with no small amount of trepidation. Snooze's owners were nice people, but she was having an increasingly difficult time thinking of entertaining anecdotes about their unsocial dachshund or glossing over the other things that had been going on around the house.

But she was a professional, so she persevered. "*Jah*, Mrs. Lee. Snooze is just fine," Grace said into the phone, hoping she sounded soothing and calm. "I know he misses you, but he seems to be doing well, all things considered."

"All things considered," Cindy Lee repeated, a new note of panic lacing her tone. "Grace, do you think Snooze knows it's Christmas and that we left him? Do you think he feels abandoned?"

Grace personally thought that Snooze didn't worry about much besides eating, sleeping, and going for a short walk in the sweater of his choice. Since that wouldn't make his owner feel very wanted, she hedged her response. "I think Snooze, ah, enjoys gazing at the beautiful tree." At least he did until John Michael had cautioned her against turning on the lights!

"I worked on those bone ornaments all year just for him."

"They are beautiful, Cindy. Truly works of art."

"Thank you. I enjoyed making them." Her voice brightened. "I could make one for you, if you'd like."

Grace bit back a chuckle. "Since we Amish don't have trees, I'm afraid that would be a waste of time. I'm surely enjoying yours, though," she added in a rush. Just in case she sounded ungrateful.

"What does Snooze do all day?"

"He sleeps a lot, of course."

"What else?" Cindy asked eagerly.

*What else?* Gazing at the lump under the blanket, Grace attempted to think of a nice way of describing the dachshund's daily activities. "He enjoys our daily walks outside," she said, glad for that. "He really enjoys wearing his sweaters."

"Which one seems to be his favorite?"

"He seems to like them all. Yesterday, he wore a jaunty red one."

Mrs. Lee chuckled. "I'm sorry. Parker just reminded me that I treat our Snooze like a child. Of course to you he is just a dog."

Since he actually was just a dog, Grace wasn't sure how to respond, but she said, "You are welcome to ask all the questions you would like. I know you love him."

"You do understand!"

"I do. Pets are part of the family." Having run out of things to say about the dachshund, she brightened her voice. "Do you have any questions about the house or anything?"

"No. Other than I hope you are staying warm. I can't believe how much snow you've been getting."

"I'm fine, thank you. Doing well."

"Okay . . . Oh! Parker says I need get off the phone and leave you in peace. We'll be back on either Christmas Day or the day after."

"Either is fine. Enjoy your vacation."

"Thank you, Grace. Good-bye!"

Just as she hung up, Snooze popped his head out of the blankets and barked. Surprised, Grace watched as he vaulted off the couch and ran to the door, barking wildly.

"I suppose I should be thankful that you waited until your mom got off the phone, Snooze," she murmured . . . right before she walked to the door to look out. "What do you hear? More squirrels chattering?"

But instead of squirrels, she saw Sheriff Brewer stepping out of his cruiser. He was talking on his radio and looking around the outside of the house.

And just like that, her body tensed and all thoughts of decorated dog bones, sweaters, and squirrels fled. She reached for the door handle, thinking to go out to meet Sheriff Brewer, but when he began pacing on the drive as he talked on the phone, she decided to wait. Snooze had snuck in front of her feet and was looking through the long window on the side of the door, too. Every couple of seconds he gave a half-hearted bark.

"Some guard dog you are, Snooze," she murmured.

After a couple more minutes passed, the sheriff at last approached the door.

She gathered Snooze in her arms and opened it before he could knock. "Sheriff Brewer, this is a surprise."

"Something happened last night that you need to know about, Miss King," he said by way of greeting. "I think we need to talk."

She felt chill bumps rise on her arms but tried to ignore them. As she ushered him inside, she said, "I have some hot coffee and some chocolate chip cookies in the kitchen. Would you like some?"

As he unzipped his jacket, he smiled at her. "I usually say no, but it's been a long day already. I'd love some."

Pleased that she could do something productive, she set Snooze down on the floor.

"He really is a cute little thing." Before she could stop him, Sheriff Brewer knelt down. "Hi, little guy. How are you?"

Snooze bared his teeth and growled before running to the couch.

The sheriff's light-blue eyes twinkled. "Is he any nicer to you?"

"Sometimes."

He laughed. "I'm starting to think pet sitters are underappreciated."

Boy, had he called that right! "Every animal has his own unique personality," she said diplomatically.

"Some more than others," he murmured.

After they got to the kitchen and she'd given him a cup of coffee and plate of cookies, she sat down across from him. "What has happened?" Grasping at straws, she said, "Did something happen to Dorma?"

"Dorma? Oh. Dorma Schultz. No. We had another robbery in the area last night. When we questioned the owners, they said that they'd thought someone had been walking around the house before. Maybe even gone inside through an unlocked window."

"Like what happened here."

"Exactly."

She felt kind of sick. "Did you catch the robbers?"

"No. But we did find out more information. It was two men. Two young men."

She thought of Dorma's nephews. "What did they take?"

"Money. Electronics. Jewelry. Just about anything that they could get their hands on." He frowned. "They did a thorough job."

"If I see more footprints, I'll let you know."

He winced. "I deserved that. I should have taken your sighting more seriously." After finishing one of the cookies on his plate, he wiped his fingers on the paper napkin placed in front of him. "Grace, they had guns."

Grace clenched her hands together, trying to stop the trembling. It didn't help. "How did you know that?"

"Because the family came home just as they were pulling away. One of the men pointed a gun at them."

Her stomach dropped. "Do you think they might come here?"

"I think it's a good possibility, Miss King. They're targeting some of the most expensive homes in the area."

Still thinking about the people getting a gun pulled on them, she swallowed. "Was the family hurt?"

"Thank the Lord, no. But Grace, I think you and that dog . . ."

"His name is Snooze."

"That you and Snooze might be in danger. Y'all need to leave and go somewhere safer."

The sheriff's words made sense, but where could she go?

Taking Snooze to her empty house didn't seem like a good option. "I don't know where else to go. This is my job. Mr. and Mrs. Lee wanted Snooze to live at home while they were out of town. I need to stay here."

"I think they'd change their tune if you were in danger."

"I think their house would be more in danger if I left."

She knew it went without saying that the Lees had a beautiful home filled with many expensive items. She couldn't in good conscience leave it empty. Then, too, she knew she wouldn't feel much safer in her empty house. Actually, she was starting to feel like she wasn't going to be safe anywhere until the burglars were caught.

Sheriff Brewer sighed and told her that he thought her priorities were messed up. When she said nothing, he looked at her steadily. "Perhaps you don't feel comfortable using the phone? I could call Mr. and Mrs. Lee if you'd like. I'd be happy to tell them about the situation around here. Explain how my deputies could drive by on a regular basis after you leave."

"If you are planning to stop by on a regular basis, then I doubt I'll have anything to worry about. Besides, as a matter of fact, I just got off the phone with Mr. and Mrs. Lee. I can talk on the phone just fine."

"You know I didn't mean to sound rude, Grace."

She exhaled. "I know. And I appreciate your care, I do. But I made a promise to the Lees, and I intend to keep it." Plus, she only had to get through another few days. Surely, she could do that?

He got to his feet. He looked strong and formidable. If she hadn't just watched him eat three cookies, she might have even been afraid of him. "There are some promises that shouldn't be kept," he said, "especially if it puts you in danger."

"I'll be fine."

He put his tan hat back on. "You look sweet and tentative, but you've got an iron will, Grace King."

She smiled at him softly. "I like how that sounds. My parents always just said that I was as stubborn as an old mule."

He chuckled. "Maybe only a young one." Rapping his knuckles on the table, he said, "You keep my number close at hand. Don't be afraid to call if you feel you are in danger."

"*Danke*, Sheriff."

He shrugged on his jacket. "I don't feel good about this, Grace. I don't feel good about it at all."

And with those parting words, he took his leave.

Making her suddenly wonder if she'd just made a very bad decision.

# CHAPTER 23

They were ten hours into another twenty-four-hour shift, and thankful that so far it had been relatively uneventful. They'd only helped a pair of new homeowners who were afraid they had a natural gas leak. John Michael was sitting at the table and eating supper.

It was his turn to do the cooking and he was proud of his efforts. He'd made beef-and-barley soup when he first got on, and put it all in a Crock-Pot to thicken and simmer over the day. He'd even brought in some of his mother's biscuits and two of her pies to finish out the meal.

"I did it," Sean said as he entered the dayroom of the station house. "My brother and I just booked a trip to Cancun. We're leaving the last week in January."

Captain Butler grinned as he got up to get another helping of soup. "Anxious for a few days at the beach, huh?"

"Oh, yeah," Sean replied with a smile. "We're going to stay at one of those all-inclusive resorts. Food, beer, fun, you name it. Can't wait."

"I always wanted to go to one of those resorts," Anderson said. "What made you decide to book it for January? I like to take my vacations in the spring."

"Do you really need to ask?" Sean said as he cut himself a generous slice of pumpkin pie. "It's been snowing like crazy, no one around here can drive in it, and we've got a pair of thieves who are starting fires for fun. I need a break."

"Shoot. When you put it like that, I think we all need a break," the captain said with a wink directed at John Michael. "I bet my wife would love to spend a couple of days running around in a bikini."

Sean chuckled. "I have a feeling you might enjoy that, too." Turning to John Michael, he said, "Any chance you could head to the beach?"

"In Mexico? *Nee,* I don't fly. But I'd like to go to the beaches in Siesta Key."

"I like Florida, too," Hank said as he got another helping of soup. "It's warm."

The bells erupted, interrupting all thoughts of vacations. Immediately, all four of them got to their feet. John Michael unplugged the Crock-Pot and put the remains of the pie back in the refrigerator, then headed down the stairs.

"We got ourselves a house fire," Captain Butler said as he scanned the information that came on the screen of his phone. "Address . . . oh, no."

Leading the way down the stairs, Sean looked at him in alarm. "What?"

"I'm pretty sure it's the address of the Amish lady you've been checking on, John Michael," Hank said as he looked at the screen on his phone, too. "It's Schultz."

Everything inside of him tensed up and before he could stop himself, John Michael shook his head. Then, remembering that whosever house they went to was a loved one of someone, guilt slid in.

Glad for his experience, he fastened his emotions down tight and picked up his turnout gear. He needed to do his job. The other men in his crew were counting on him. That was what he needed to concentrate on. God would take care of the rest.

The captain had been right. The fire was at Dorma's, and when they arrived, the front of her small house was engulfed in flames. The moment Hank pulled to a stop, the captain started calling out orders.

Training kicked in. John's face mask was on and fastened tight, his breathing apparatus running. And he was completely focused on obeying his captain's directives.

Within seconds, hoses were pulled, the hydrant was being hooked up, and Hank was at the side panel, monitoring the amount of water and its pressure. Once again, the first rush of power made John take a step back as his muscles acclimated to the power.

Next to him, Anderson did the same thing, then motioned him forward.

Though he wished he could be out in front, following the captain into the burning building, he knew he was needed manning the hose.

He was vaguely aware of the sheriff's cruiser coming to a stop and Noah Freeman's team pulling up in the ambulance.

"Steady now," the captain called out.

"On it," John Michael said into the microphone attached to his face shield and helmet. He held firm, carefully spraying the source of the flames as he'd been taught.

And quietly reciting the Lord's Prayer to himself.

Two minutes passed, then he heard the captain's voice. "We got her. She's out but breathing." He called out a couple of more codes, but John Michael barely heard. All he could do was stare at the building. Hoping and praying for both the captain, Sean, and Dorma to appear.

When they did, he felt like he could breathe at last.

"Let's get this done," Hank called out, motioning John Michael to the building, which was now only smoking.

His heart sank as he realized that the building was ruined. There would be no saving it—or any of the things that Dorma had been so fond of.

Remembering how she'd showed them her grandmother's quilt and a wall hanging that her mother had made, he felt sad. She had been precariously holding on to her memories. Clinging to things like the hanging and the quilt. Now they were all gone.

"We're good. The fire's out," Hank called out. "I'm shutting it down."

While Sean and the captain went back into the building, which was now only a mess of burnt wood and ashes, Hank loped down to the hydrant to disconnect the line. John Michael pulled his face mask up and looked around the scene as he started to wind up the hoses.

There was a good crowd around them. Some were staring at the captain and Sean enter the building; others were watching the EMTs load Dorma into the ambulance.

Several others were around the sheriff. He was calmly answering questions and cautioning everyone to stay back and to keep out of the way.

Almost a half an hour later, most of the men were gathered around the truck and unfastening the toggles on their coats. "We did good, men," the captain said. "We got her out."

"I'm just glad she wasn't struggling to breathe," Sean said. "It made our jobs a little easier."

"Did y'all notice how she was holding on to that box?" Anderson said. "I can't believe out of everything inside there, that's what she grabbed."

"Grace told me that it contains some special letters inside," John Michael supplied.

Captain Butler's expression softened. "We saved two important things, then," he said with a smile.

John Michael tried to concentrate on the positives. They'd gotten to Dorma's in time to pull her to safety. The preliminary reports were that she was going to be fine. None of the men on his crew were hurt. There were many blessings for which to be thankful for.

But he couldn't help but wonder what was going to happen to Dorma Schultz next.

And how that fire had started. Had she had an accident . . . or had it been set on purpose like so many others in the area?

For the first time, he almost didn't want to know the answer.

# CHAPTER 24

Grace had never been so grateful for both the Lees' telephone and the availability of English drivers. From the moment John Michael called to tell her about the fire at Miss Dorma's house, she'd been anxious to see her.

The Lord had obviously been on her side, because Grace had gotten to the hospital less than an hour after she'd received John Michael's call. Now all she had to do was hope and pray that Miss Dorma would make a full recovery.

"May I help you?" the receptionist asked.

After giving her name and Dorma's, Grace was taken to a small curtained area just off the reception area.

"Miraculously, Miss Schultz hasn't sustained any serious injuries," the nurse said as she escorted Grace down the hall. "The doctors and nurses treated a few minor scratches and have had her on oxygen, but she is responding well. She should be able to be released within a few hours."

"That is wonderful-*gut*," Grace replied. "*Wonderbaar.*" Realizing she'd been speaking Pennsylvania Dutch, she shook her head as if to clear it. "I'm sorry. I guess I'm real rattled. I mean that is good news."

"I understood you. My grandmother is Amish," the nurse said with a smile. "And for the record, I completely agree." After they passed two more curtained areas, they stopped. "Dorma is back here." After pulling back the blue curtain, she escorted Grace into the small area.

To her surprise, Dorma wasn't in a hospital gown. She was dressed in her regular clothes and was even sitting up in bed. She had a cozy-looking blanket across her lap and an oxygen tube inserted in her nose.

She also smiled when she saw her. "You came to visit," she said after the nurse checked her vitals and left.

"Of course I did," she said as she rushed to her side. "I came the moment I heard about your accident."

Her smile faded. "Accident?"

Worry bubbled up inside of Grace. Was Dorma so confused she didn't even remember what had happened? "Yes," Grace said slowly. "Do you remember the accident at your home?"

Dorma shook her head. "*Nee.* I only remember the fire."

Grace sat down in the one chair by the bed. "That's what I'm speaking of," she said gently. Instead of dwelling on how the fire started, she decided it would be better to concentrate on the positives. "I'm mighty glad you weren't injured too badly. I was worried about you!"

Looking more coherent than usual, Dorma gripped the blanket over her legs. "It was scary. I was looking at my letters when I smelled smoke. At first I thought I was imagining things, but I wasn't." Her voice quivered. "And then the flames got bigger and bigger. I didn't know what to do. All I knew to do was hold on to my box of letters and pray."

Grace covered Miss Dorma's hand with both of her own. "I would have been frightened, too." Eyeing the cherrywood box, she said, "And you even saved your letters!"

"I wouldn't leave them."

"I am proud of you," Grace said softly. "And the Lord was looking out for you, too! John Michael and the other firemen got there and saved you."

"*Jah.* The men carried me out of the house." Looking sad, she added, "Everything is gone but my letters."

"We'll worry about that tomorrow. Today is for giving thanks."

Dorma nodded. With a cough, she leaned back against her

pillow. After Grace helped her take a sip of water, Dorma said, "I don't know how the fire started. It happened fast."

Grace wasn't sure what the right thing to say was. Should she redirect the conversation so she wouldn't get even more flustered? Or let her speak about what was on her mind?

Hesitantly, she said, "Did you leave something on the stove?"

"*Nee.*"

"Maybe a candle knocked over? Or something happened with a kerosene light?"

"After the firemen came, we changed everything to batteries. I don't use candles anymore. Only flashlights. The same with kerosene light." Looking perplexed, she said, "I don't know how it started, but I didn't do it."

Grace racked her mind. "Did you clean out your fireplace? Sometimes, hot ashes or coals can start a fire."

"*Nee,* Grace. I did none of those things. I didn't make the fire."

Miss Dorma sounded so sure. So coherent. She didn't want to argue with her, but Grace knew how absent-minded and confused Dorma was now. Though it could have been set by the arsonists, Grace feared this one might have been set on accident by Dorma.

But no matter what was the cause, she knew this wasn't the time to talk about it. "Let's not talk about it anymore," she soothed. "You need to rest."

"*Nee.*" Her voice sounded frantic. "It's important, Grace."

"I agree. But it already happened. We can't go back in time, right?" she said gently. "The fire investigators will figure out what happened and let us know."

Continuing to become agitated, she nodded. "I hope so."

The curtain shifted, bringing in a doctor, a nurse, and John Michael.

"Looks like you have someone looking after you, Dorma," the doctor said. Turning to Grace, he held out his hand. "I'm Dr. Metzger."

After smiling quickly at John Michael, she shook the doctor's hand. "I'm Grace King."

"Grace, I'm glad you're here to help with our patient." Turning back to Dorma, he said, "How are you feeling?"

"I can breathe better."

"That's good," he said with a warm smile. He looked over at John Michael and Grace. "We're going to check her lungs again. If you could step outside."

"I'll be right back," Grace said as she walked to John Michael's side and left the room. After they walked a little farther down the way, she smiled at him. "Hiya. I didn't expect to see you here."

"I'm not supposed to be. I'm in the middle of my shift. I asked if someone could come in and finish my hours, though. I wasn't about to leave Miss Dorma alone."

"I'm so glad you were able to do that."

"Me, too. The captain was real understanding." Pointing to another door, he said, "I was just on the phone with the other guys at the firehouse. Everyone is real worried about her. She looked pretty frightened when the EMTs loaded her into the ambulance."

"That's so kind of them all."

He smiled. "We tend to feel pretty protective about people we rescue." Stepping closer, he reached out and ran his hand down her arm. "I'm glad you got here so fast! A little amazed, too. I didn't think I'd see you for another hour."

"I was able to get a ride right away." When she gazed up at him, she realized that he didn't smell faintly of smoke like Dorma did. "Are you all right? I didn't even ask."

"I'm fine. I took a shower at the station before I came over here. I'm as good as new."

"Was the fire terrible? I mean, all fires are terrible, but was it small or large?"

"It was a good one, but we contained it quickly enough. Her house is gone, of course. However, no other houses were damaged, which is something to be thankful for."

Just imagining the scene, Grace shivered. "So, you said that the fire started in the kitchen? Are you sure?"

"It's going to take a while for the investigators to make a report.

But it seems a good guess that she left something on the stove or there was a grease fire or something."

"Miss Dorma said she hadn't been cooking."

"No offense to her, but we both know Miss Dorma is pretty confused. She probably doesn't remember."

"Usually I would agree, but she seemed certain that the fire wasn't her fault."

John Michael gazed at her thoughtfully. "I guess we'll have to wait to see what the report says."

"*Jah.*"

The nurse popped her head out into the hall. "The doctor has cleared Miss Schultz. She can leave soon. Will she be leaving with both of y'all?"

"*Nee,*" John Michael answered. "Actually—"

"She'll be coming home with me," Grace interjected firmly.

"Grace—"

"I've made up my mind, John." Though it was difficult, she ignored John Michael's grunt of dismay.

This was the right thing to do. There was no way she was going to let some stranger look after Miss Dorma, or whatever John Michael had planned. For now, at least, Miss Dorma was her responsibility—for better or worse.

# CHAPTER 25

Though Grace had done a good job of acting like she was completely in control, John Michael knew she was shaken up. Her expression was strained, and she hardly said a word, almost like if she relaxed too much, she was going to dissolve into tears.

Or maybe he was the one who was about to lose it.

Grace had taken him completely by surprise when she told the nurse she was going to take Dorma home with her. He wasn't sure if that was the best option, but since he'd been planning to ask his parents to take Dorma in until they could find someone else, he didn't argue with her.

But that didn't mean he wasn't going to try to help Grace as much as he could! He was worried about her heaping so much on her shoulders and never asking for help. He guessed she was afraid of looking weak, but he already thought she was pretty incredible. She didn't have to do anything more to raise her esteem in his eyes.

He stayed by her side for three hours, helping her sign the discharge forms, arranging transportation for all three of them, and finally assisting with getting Miss Dorma into the Lees' house.

He'd already talked to some of the hospital staff about Dorma's need for clothing and basic necessities. The nurse who'd been monitoring Dorma told them that she had Amish relatives and contacts and would take care of getting some things sent to Dorma. She somehow also managed to find a plain gray dress for Dorma to wear out of the hospital, since her clothing smelled like smoke.

Once they arrived at the Lees' house, John Michael helped Grace deflect all of Miss Dorma's questions about why she was going to be staying in an Englisher's home instead of with another Amish family in the county. He followed Grace's lead, helping the older woman get settled in one of the bedrooms and bringing her hot tea and a scone.

He'd even done a good job of holding back his amusement when Snooze hopped into bed next to Dorma, much to Grace's dismay.

Now he was sitting on one of the barstools in the fancy kitchen, watching Grace make chicken noodle soup. She seemed flustered and worried.

John Michael figured there were at least five reasons she could be feeling that way. But he had learned something over the last couple of days in her company. Pressuring and bullying her didn't help. Grace was a hard worker and independent. She also had a softness, a vulnerability about her that could easily bruise. He didn't want to hurt her in any way.

But he would be lying if he said he didn't think the events of the week weren't going to get the best of her soon. She'd taken on a lot—maybe more than she realized.

After she added the chopped carrots, celery, and onions to the broth, Grace set down her wooden spoon. "I'm guessing you have a lot to say to me about taking on such a responsibility like Dorma."

Before this week, he probably would have blurted exactly what was on his mind. But he was finally starting to learn that caring for someone didn't just mean taking care of them. It was also listening to and supporting them, even when he didn't always agree with their actions. "I'd rather you tell me."

Before his eyes, she seemed to stand a little straighter. "I just think she needs someone, John Michael. She needs someone who really cares to help her right now."

"I agree."

"I know you could have asked your parents to take her in, or to talk to the preachers and the bishop. But other than a couple of people dropping off groceries, it doesn't seem enough." She shook her head sadly. "Every time I think of how messy her kitchen and bedroom were the first time I visited, I want to cry."

"Her house was in a bad state, that is true."

She continued as if he hadn't said a word. "I mean, no one has really been there for her. Why should I expect anyone else to step in now?" She frowned. "And what if Miss Dorma doesn't trust them? That would make things worse, don'tcha think?"

When she paused to catch her breath, he said, "Are you asking for my opinion or just wondering aloud?"

She blinked before smiling sheepishly. "I don't know."

"How about this, then? I think all of your reasons for bringing her here are *gut*. I also don't think you are wrong. Dorma has needed help for some time now. She can't live alone any longer."

Grace looked at him intently. All that emotion and wonder he'd always loved in those gray-green eyes came out in full force. "You think so?"

He had to take a sip of water so his voice wouldn't be filled with emotion. "Oh, *jah*. As far as I can see, there's only one problem."

"And what is that?"

He decided to tackle the obvious. "This isn't your house, and you're going to be moving back home soon. Then what are you going to do with Dorma?"

And just like that, all of the excitement that had been shining in her eyes faded slightly. "I've been thinking about that, too. And I think I've come up with a plan."

"What is that?"

She held up a hand. "Don't laugh."

"I won't." Now he was really charmed. She was so cute and earnest! He was also plenty curious.

And, if he was honest, a little apprehensive, too. But, remembering his new intention of listening to her, he nodded encouragingly.

"I'm going to get my own place and move in with Dorma."

He hesitated. She was so young. Dorma had an affliction that was obviously going to get worse. Neither of them had any idea about her financial situation.

And, then . . . there were all the things he'd been feeling. He wanted to court her. He was now certain that she was the one for him. But how could a future for the two of them happen in such a situation?

And what kind of a man was he if he was putting all of his selfish reasons ahead of Miss Dorma's needs?

But because he was still trying really hard to be a listener instead of an advisor, he only murmured, "You want to become Miss Dorma's caregiver."

Looking hesitant, she nodded. "I've been a pet sitter for a long time and have saved a lot of money. I can afford to rent my own place. John Michael, I know I sound naïve, but I feel strongly about this. Even though I never planned on being a caregiver, I think it is the best thing for me to do. I love her, John Michael."

"Ah." Really, he should get an award for keeping so closed-mouthed.

Then, at last it came. "What do you think?"

Here was his chance! But suddenly, all of his objections and logical concerns seemed wrong. Who was he to say what she should do? "I think I'm real proud of you, Grace. I think if you want to do all of these things, I want to help you."

She looked skeptical. "Really? That's all you're going to say?"

"What? You wanted me to tell you something different?"

"*Nee* . . . but I guess I thought you'd tell me that I am too young or I don't know what I am getting into."

"Maybe you are too young. Maybe you don't know what you are getting into." He got off the stool and walked toward her. "But I don't know if that's a bad thing."

"How?"

"Isn't that what faith is? We believe in the unknown? We go forward, knowing that the Lord has our back and that He's leading us on this path in the first place?"

"I hope so. I hope He's leading me on this path. I can't do it alone, John."

"Of course not." Unable to help himself, he reached out and took hold of both of her hands, which were hanging loosely down by her sides. "I don't think it's a coincidence that you met Dorma at Christmas. I also don't think it's a coincidence that we reunited while you were here at the Lees' house. I think He's been working through us this whole time. And what's more, I'm thankful for His help."

"I'm thankful for His help, too. And for yours, John Michael. If I didn't have you, I would've never pushed myself to do this."

He lowered his voice. "Don't you see, Grace? I want to help you, too. I'm not going to let you try to handle everything alone."

"Because Dorma means so much to you, too?"

"*Nee*, Silly. Because you do."

And then, while she stared up at him in wonder, he finally did what he'd been wanting to do for the last several days. He pulled her closer, curved his arms around her, and kissed Grace King.

# CHAPTER 26

To Grace's shame, she'd waited a whole ten seconds before pulling away. And when she did? . . . well, she felt that loss so
deeply, she wished she could turn back time and kiss John Michael again.

She settled for holding on to his arms and gazing up at him.

John Michael looked just as taken aback as she did. His expression a little stunned and, yes, a little heated.

At least he wasn't unaffected! Slowly, she smiled.

Which made him blink. "Ah, Grace . . . have I just ruined everything between us? Do I need to apologize?"

She swallowed. "Do you want to apologize?"

"Definitely not." He ran two fingertips along her cheek, his eyes
watching the move. "You may never have wanted to hear me say
this, but I've been wanting to kiss you for quite a while. Actually,
for a very long time."

He'd just said the words that she'd been thinking. Back when
she was just a child, she'd imagined him being her first kiss.
Though she wasn't now exactly experienced, she had kissed two
other men, both of those experiences might as well have been brief
handshakes. That's how much emotion she was feeling in comparison. Her mouth went dry as she realized that she probably
needed to say something to relieve his worries. Maybe it would
be best for her to mumble something demure. If she did that,
Grace knew John Michael wouldn't press her. He would likely

drop his hand, step back, and start talking about the weather or something.

Or . . . she could continue to show him that she was no longer a little girl. And since God had decided that today was the day she started making adult decisions, Grace knew there was only one thing to do. "I've wanted to kiss you for some time, as well," she murmured.

His expression warmed as his fingertips curved around her neck, then traipsed down to stop in between her shoulder blades. "And?"

She laughed. "And that's all I'm going to say about that." She might be all grown up now, but she wasn't brash!

To her pleasure, John Michael seemed more amused. "I do believe you are going to keep me on my toes, Grace."

"I hope so."

Just as she was sure he was going to kiss her again, his phone buzzed.

Looking regretful, he pulled it out of his pocket. "Sorry, Grace. It's Captain Butler."

She watched as he pressed some buttons and held the phone to his ear. "John Michael here."

Feeling at a loss, she walked back to the stove. After tasting her soup, she added a pinch more salt and continued to eye him as he talked. As the minutes passed, John Michael kept edging farther away and speaking in lower tones. Soon she couldn't hear a single word he was saying.

When he at last clicked off, he walked back to her side. "I'm sorry, Grace. I need to go."

"I hope there's not an emergency?"

"No, nothing like that. Just a meeting the captain would like me to attend. And since I was supposed to be on duty anyway, I need to get on my way."

"How will you get there?" Arriving at the house, they'd paid and let the driver from the hospital go.

"Anderson, one of the guys I work with, is almost here. I need to grab my coat and meet him outside. But I'll call you later, okay?"

"Okay. Sure," she said, attempting to give him a reassuring smile. She didn't think he saw it, though.

As she heard him open and then shut the front door, Grace turned the soup on low and wandered into the living room. Snooze popped into view walking from Dorma's room toward his cozy spot on the couch. When he sauntered to her side, she bent down to pick him up; and when he gave her a lick, she felt tears form in her eyes. Maybe he realized just how much she needed that.

"Ach, Snooze. What am I doing? I'm adopting a woman I hardly know and kissing men in other people's kitchens! These things aren't like me at all. Honestly, I feel like my life is swirling and drifting about like snowflakes in an early winter storm."

Staring at her intently, Snooze tilted his head to one side. Fancifully, she answered his unspoken question.

"Well, yes, I think I do know what I want. I want John Michael and Dorma in my life. And . . . and I want John Michael to one day love me, just like I know I'm starting to love him."

Snooze whined.

Nodding her head, she said, "I agree. Beth is going to hate me if I fall in love with John Michael. And I might fail at taking care of Dorma. I know nothing about caring for the elderly or dementia."

When Snooze stared at her intently, Grace swallowed. "I agree. I would love to only think about what *I* want. But doing that isn't always the best thing to do. You see, sometimes a person can want too much."

Snooze closed his eyes.

It seemed the dog had given up on her. Maybe he was right and she was hopeless!

Looking at the Lees' Christmas tree, she tried to relax. Eventually, Snooze started to squirm. Knowing that he needed to get some exercise, she set him on the ground, turned off the burner, put on her coat, fastened his leash, and took him outside.

The weather had warmed over the last twenty-four hours, creating rivulets of water in the lawn. Snooze's paws sank through the melting snow and made his belly get wet, too.

He looked thoroughly disgruntled and she didn't blame him. "I'm sorry, Snooze. It's a dog's burden to do his business outside. In every other instance, you have an easy time of it."

He growled, then stuck his nose to the ground and sniffed. Dutifully, she tromped through the snow as well, her mind on John Michael, the meeting he was headed to, and Miss Dorma sleeping upstairs.

As Snooze continued to sniff and trudge through the snow, she let her mind drift, thinking about all the events that had led to this point. Snooze taking off. John Michael helping her. Seeing Miss Dorma in the diner. The accidents, the fires, the need to do something to help herself and others.

She knew God didn't make mistakes, but she sure wished He sometimes offered explanations, too. It seemed like an awful lot was going on when everyone should be concentrating on the miracle of Jesus's birth.

When Snooze barked, signaling that he was more than ready to return to the house, she scooped him up in her arms and hurried back inside. Then she made a cup of peppermint tea, turned on the gas fireplace, and settled on the couch to take a nap—

Just as the phone rang.

"Hello?" she said eagerly, hoping that it was John Michael but knowing that was unlikely.

"Grace! It's so *gut* to hear your voice."

"Jennifer?" Oh, but this was the best surprise! Tears pricked her eyes at the sound of her friend's voice. "It is so good to hear from you. How is your trip?"

"Good. I've been spending time with my cousin Anna, whose next-door neighbor is both friendly and cute. His name is Kevin."

Leave it to Jennifer to lay things out so neatly! "I'm jealous. It sounds as if you are having a Christmas romance."

"Maybe. Now, what about you?"

"Oh, where to start?"

"That sounds ominous."

"It feels ominous. I've had quite the adventure here."

"Start talking. I want to hear all about it."

"I'll share it when you get back. You're in a phone shanty, ain't so?"

"*Jah.* How about the short version?"

Grace smiled, then blurted out the most important parts. "I've reconnected with Miss Dorma Schultz. Do you remember her?"

"*Jah.* Vaguely."

"Well, she had a fire at her house and now she's living with me. In addition, Snooze and I connected with John Michael Miller."

"Wait! Isn't he your sister's old boyfriend?"

"Yes, he is."

"How does he look?"

That was why she loved Jennifer. She asked the things Grace would be embarrassed to tell anyone else. "He looks *gut.* Handsome."

"Is he really a firefighter?"

"Oh, yes. He was one of the men to rescue Miss Dorma."

"So he's a hero."

"He is. But he's more than that."

"More than a hero?" Jennifer sucked in a breath. "Grace, has something happened between the two of you?"

Feeling her cheeks blush, she continued on. "I've come to realize that the infatuation I felt for him was not one-sided." Yes, that was a rather wordy way of saying it, but her head felt just that jumbled!

"Wait a minute," Jennifer said. "Are you saying that he likes you, too?"

She couldn't resist smiling. "Oh, *jah.*"

"How did you know? Did he tell you?"

"He did." After the briefest of pauses, she blurted, "He also kissed me."

"Where?"

"Where? On the mouth."

Jennifer burst out laughing. "Oh, Grace. Only you would take that question so literally. I meant where were you two when this big event happened?" Her voice lowered. "Was it somewhere romantic? Had he taken you for a sleigh ride?"

Okay, now it was really good they were talking on the phone instead of sitting across from each other, because her face had to be beet red from both embarrassment and humor. "*Nee*, it wasn't anyplace that romantic. He kissed me here in the kitchen."

Jennifer's sighed. "I suppose romance can happen anywhere." Before Grace could comment on that, Jennifer continued. "So, what are you going to do now?"

"I don't know. Everything is such a mess. Then, too, there have been burglaries in the area and lots of fires, too."

"Plus, Christmas is on its way," Jennifer added.

"Yes. Like I said, I can hardly keep up."

"Fires and love and danger and rescues," mused Jennifer. "It reminds me of all those promises the Lord made in Isaiah, doesn't it?"

Jennifer's family loved to memorize and quote verses. She easily knew three times more Bible verses than Grace did. "I don't know what verse that is."

"You'll have to look it up. It's Isaiah forty-something, I can't remember," she said in a rush. "But in any case, it's all about how you won't be burned when you walk through fires."

"I have a feeling they weren't talking about literal fires, Jen."

"Maybe I'm not, either. Oops! My uncle needs the phone. I'll see you soon! Merry Christmas."

"*Jah*, Merry Christmas," Grace said as she heard the phone click.

Then she sipped the tea, cuddled Snooze, and stared into the fireplace as she made a mental note to look up that verse soon.

She had a feeling she was going to need to glean that meaning as soon as possible. She was going to need all the help she could get.

# CHAPTER 27

Isaiah 43:2. *'When you pass through the waters, I will be with you; and when you pass through the rivers, they will not sweep over you. When you walk through the fire, you will not be burned; the flame will not set you ablaze.'"*

Grace paused, then read it aloud again, emphasizing different words this time. It all sounded very dark and meaningful. And, perhaps, confusing. She felt a burst of nervousness as she placed her finger on each word on the Bible's page. She felt as if God and Jennifer were telling her something very important. But what was she supposed to learn, exactly?

Annoyed with her suddenly slow-functioning brain, she read it out loud a third time.

"Did you walk through the fire, Grace?" Dorma asked from the hallway.

Flustered, Grace hastily closed the Bible. "Miss Dorma, you surprised me! I didn't expect you to wake up yet. How are you feeling?"

Dorma shrugged off her concern. Instead, she asked the question again. "Did you walk through fire?"

"*Nee.* I did not. But you did." Struggling to regain her composure, Grace went toward Dorma, hoping to take her hand. "Remember, you had the fire, not me. And John Michael walked through the fire, too. He is the fireman, *jah*? He and his friends helped save you."

Walking toward her, Dorma nodded. "He did, but that isn't of what you speak."

Grace paused, unsure if they were talking about the same things, then mentally shrugged her shoulders. What did it even matter, especially if talking about the verse with somebody else could only help? "You're right," she said slowly. "It isn't. I'm speaking of other fires. The types of fires one can't see or feel." Brightening her voice, she continued. "Now, how about something to eat? I made chicken noodle soup." She curved her hand around Dorma's elbow. "Let's go into the kitchen."

Dorma walked compliantly by her side, but she was gazing blankly around her.

Grace's spirits sagged. Dorma had acted so alert, Grace had started hoping that her condition was improving. Obviously, that wasn't the case. Gently, Grace asked, "Do you remember that we are at the Lees' *haus* now?"

"*Jah.*"

"That's *gut*. Remember, we're going to be staying—"

Dorma interrupted her. "We are walking through our own fires now."

Grace stopped. "Wait, you're still thinking about that verse, aren't you?"

"The Lord gives each of us fires and floods. Some are large and some are small."

"It certainly does feel like that, doesn't it?" said Grace. "But He doesn't make mistakes, so I guess we're supposed to go through them. Luckily, John Michael works for the fire department," she teased.

Dorma stopped and pressed a hand to her arm. "You mustn't forget the rest of it, Grace."

"What is that?"

"That He promised He would help us through," Dorma said as she pulled away from Grace's grip, strode over to the kitchen table, sat down, and primly set her hands in her lap. Then, just as if she was sitting in a fancy restaurant, she looked at Grace directly in the eye. "I would like soup now."

Pulling a bowl out of a cabinet, Grace smiled. "Then I think you should have some."

LATE THAT AFTERNOON, John Michael returned to the Lees' house. But this time he had Captain Butler and Sheriff Brewer with him. Grace was used to the men's visits now and didn't feel too alarmed at the sight of them.

After they exchanged greetings and she took the men's coats and set them on the back of a chair, Sheriff Brewer said, "We need to speak with you, Grace. Well, with you and Dorma."

Feeling dread in the pit of her stomach, she led them into the living room. "Dorma is upstairs. Do you need me to go fetch her right now?" She kind of hoped they would first tell her what they wanted, then she could help deliver the news to Dorma.

But that wasn't the case.

"*Jah.* You'd best go get her right now," John Michael said.

Just as she started upstairs, she could practically feel the men's eyes dart to the dry Christmas tree. "Don't worry," she said with a smile. "I'm still filling the tree's container with water and not turning on its lights."

Captain Butler looked relieved. "That's good, but I have to tell you that it's not safe this close to the fire. If a stray spark hits it, that tree could burst into flames before you are even aware what's happening."

Turning to John, she asked, "Would you help me move the tree farther away from the fireplace?"

"That's a real *gut* idea," John Michael said. Getting to his feet, he turned to the other men. "How about if we move the tree to the back corner of the room?"

The captain and sheriff looked pleased to help, and they all crouched around the tree as she walked up the stairs.

After coming to terms that she was going to be vacuuming up

needles all afternoon, she worried once again about the purpose of their visit.

It was obvious that they weren't here just to check on her and Dorma. Something was definitely going on and it was serious. She'd seen John Michael wear many moods. She now recognized his glower when he was irritated with her but trying hard not to let it show.

She saw his patience when he was with Dorma, repeating the same words over and over when she was confused. His energy when he was working outside, a flirty side when he sat with her the other night and kissed her so sweetly.

But everything he was exhibiting now was new to her. He seemed pensive and tense. Tightly wound up and nervous.

After knocking softly on Dorma's door, she peeked in.

Dorma was sitting in the big easy chair next to the window and gazing out into the snow. In her lap were four magazines that Grace had given her. They were Christmas catalogs and a *Better Homes and Gardens*. Mrs. Lee had received them two days ago. Usually, Grace would never think of touching one of her clients' mail, but she'd made an exception. Dorma seemed to enjoy looking at the pages over and over again. Perhaps it was a calming influence.

Grace figured Dorma needed as many activities as possible that could ease her nerves.

"Do you have another book?" Dorma asked.

"*Nee.* I wish." She paused, then gave her the news as gently as possible. "John Michael and some other men are here. They want to speak to us both."

Her eyes widened. "Because of the fire?"

"*Jah.* I mean, I think that's the reason. They didn't actually tell me why they came." Crossing the room, she helped Dorma get to her feet and smooth out her gray dress and apron.

Then they went down to hear what the men had to say. She figured it was silly, but she hoped they were finally getting some good news at last.

# CHAPTER 28

After they greeted Dorma and everyone sat down, John Michael knew they couldn't put off the news any longer. The other men, thinking that Dorma might need to be talked to in Pennsylvania Dutch, had agreed to let him start the discussion. "We got the report from the fire investigator, Dorma," he said quietly.

"I did not set the fire," she said in an almost defiant tone of voice. "I was looking at my letters."

"We believe you," Captain Butler said. "Someone doused a cardboard box with an accelerant, set it on the back doorstep by the kitchen, and lit it on fire. That's how the fire started. Everyone knows you were not to blame."

Grace's eyes widened. "That is terrible! Dorma could have gotten badly injured or worse. Why would someone do such a thing?"

Captain Butler nodded. "Exactly."

Grace shivered. "That's horrible."

"It is," John Michael agreed, wishing he could wrap an arm around her. "But luckily, they've started getting sloppy and began to make mistakes."

"Did they even realize Dorma was in her home?" She jumped to her feet. "She could've died."

John Michael walked to Grace's side. "I know you're upset, but you aren't helping Dorma," he murmured. "She needs you to be calm right now."

Grace glanced over to the older woman. She had wrapped her arms around her middle and was staring at them in concern.

"I'm sorry everyone," Grace announced. "I . . . well, I guess I just let the stress of it all get the best of me."

John Michael took her hand. "Let's sit down. There's more information to share."

After the others sat back down, Sheriff Brewer spoke.

"Here's what we know so far. At the beginning, I think they tried to be careful. They scoped out houses, looking for ones that had a lot of valuables, places that would be worth their time."

"We now think that's what happened with you, Grace," Captain Butler shared. "Someone was watching the Lees' home, they saw you run off after Snooze, so they used the opportunity to look inside."

John Michael nodded, "When you went for a long walk the other day, they probably were going to get started, but then you came back early."

Grace's eyes widened. "Someone's been watching me?" When Sheriff Brewer nodded, she added, "But that doesn't make sense. We found those tracks several days ago. No one has been back. At least I don't think they have."

"I don't know why they haven't come back," the sheriff said, frustration thick in his tone. "Things like this have been going on all over the county. At first, we thought only some areas were being targeted, but now the pattern has become more erratic."

"The things we have learned haven't been especially helpful, either," Captain Butler continued. "Sometimes they target a big place like this to rob. Other times, it's a small home like the one two houses down from Dorma's."

"The Franks were robbed during Dorma's fire," John Michael said. Two days ago, an Amish home out near Cub Run was burned and an English house at the end of that same street was robbed.

Grace now looked even more apprehensive. She reached for Dorma's hand. "I thought I was doing the right thing by bringing her here."

Sheriff Brewer got to his feet. "Everyone at the sheriff's office is beyond frustrated. Our resources are getting low and my deputies are getting stretched to the limit," he said slowly. "Plus, there have been other matters to see to besides these robberies and fires. I would like to tell you that I can ensure your safety here, but I'm afraid that's impossible."

"Of course you can't promise that," Grace said slowly. "None of us can predict the future."

John Michael breathed a sigh of relief. Maybe she was finally going to be open to some other options.

"How can I help? What should I do?" she asked.

"I need you to be even more alert and keep your eyes open. If you see anything suspicious at all, I want you to call us immediately."

Grace nodded. "I can do that."

Still on his feet, Sheriff Brewer continued. "I got on the phone and called the departments in other counties and asked if any of their men or women could help us out. That will help with patrols, and with tracking down the guys who are doing this . . . but until then, I'm worried about you and Dorma being here alone. Is there someone who could stay here with you?"

After darting a glance John Michael's way, she said, "I'm not sure."

Unable to help himself John Michael said, "Wouldn't it be better if she left?"

Before the sheriff answered, Grace shook her head. "Houses everywhere are getting targeted. Who's to say Dorma and I would be safer someplace else?" She lowered her voice. "Besides, I don't want to only concentrate on our safety. I need to consider what is best for Dorma. She's finally settled. She's sleeping and eating again. And she's calmer and more at peace. That's important, too."

John Michael knew she had a point. Every person in the county couldn't abandon their home just in case something terrible might happen. They needed to continue to live their lives and care for the people they loved. And for Grace, that included Dorma.

Just as she was leaning back against the cushions on the couch, Snooze pattered into the room. After eyeing them all, he trotted toward her and looked up. Grace leaned down to carefully rub his back.

Then, to John's surprise, Snooze got up on his hind legs and pressed his tiny front paws on her thigh. A tender smile appeared on Grace's face. She picked the pup up and held him in her lap.

Then Grace turned to John Michael and smiled.

There was so much love and affection in her eyes for that little dog that he knew exactly what he was going to do.

"Actually, Grace does know someone who could stay here with her. Me."

When Grace smiled at him, he realized that was what she'd been hoping for all along.

"That sounds like the best solution," Sheriff Brewer said. "Even with extra manpower, we can't be everywhere at once. I'll feel better knowing that Dorma and Grace won't be here alone all the time."

Captain Butler grinned at her. "You're collecting houseguests left and right, Miss King."

Looking pleased as punch, she looked directly at John Michael. "Indeed, I am."

# CHAPTER 29

Feeling both exhilarated and confused by the meeting, Grace knew she couldn't simply sit on the couch. John had left a few minutes after the men and promised to return as soon as his shift was over. Now she needed some fresh air, and thought Snooze probably did, too.

She helped the dachshund into another sweater—this one cranberry-colored—fastened his leash, and invited Dorma to take the short walk with them.

To Grace's delight, Dorma didn't hesitate. As if she'd owned them for years, she slipped on the thick wool cloak and warm boots that the nurse from the hospital had dropped off a few hours ago.

"I used to walk my dog Charlie every morning," she said as Grace fastened her cloak and ushered all of them out the door.

"I didn't know you used to have a dog," Grace said as they walked down the drive toward the mailbox, stopping often for Snooze to sniff.

"Oh, *jah*. She was a black cocker spaniel."

"Named Charlie?" Hoping to encourage Dorma to talk some more, she said, "Charlie is a boy's name."

"It wasn't a common name for a spaniel," Dorma agreed. "But I always liked the name. My Abraham and I had always wanted to name our son that."

Grace smiled at her. Right at the moment, Miss Dorma was looking like her old self. Her eyes were shining and her face was flushed with happiness. She even seemed to be enjoying the walk, not having any trouble keeping up with Grace and Snooze's steady pace. "When did your husband pass on to heaven, Miss Dorma?"

"Oh, it's been many years ago now, child. He passed when your John Michael was still a boy."

Even though she knew Dorma didn't mean anything by the remark, Grace still felt herself blush. "He's not my John Michael."

"Oh?" Her gray eyes lit with amusement. "If he's not yours, then whose is he?"

"What?" she sputtered around a laugh. "My stars, I surely don't know."

"I think you might, child," Dorma said with a small smile.

Grace would have protested again if she hadn't been so happy to see the difference in Dorma's manner. She seemed so much more vibrant and observant, like a sheet had been pulled off of her and she could finally be her true self. Grace wondered if it was the change of scenery, the fact that she wasn't alone, or if that was how her mind worked now.

Of course, the reason didn't matter. What did was that Dorma seemed happier.

"I bet John Michael was cute when he was a small boy," Grace murmured, unable to stop herself.

"He was mischievous, that's what he was. He was always into something. His *mamm* always claimed that he could never sit still for more than an hour and couldn't stop talking for more than a minute."

Grace chuckled. "That sounds about right." Thinking of his job and what little she knew about it, she said, "Maybe that's why he became a fireman. I can't see him only working by himself on a farm day after day."

"Maybe. I don't know. Only the Lord knows."

"Yes, that is true." They continued to walk, the snow crunching under their feet.

Snooze, looking snug in his sweater, stopped every couple of feet to take a bite of snow or bark at a squirrel in the distance.

Their little walk felt peaceful and right. She wasn't sure what was going to happen in the future, but Grace was happy to have these few moments. They felt heaven-sent. "Did you understand that John Michael is going to be staying with the two of us and Snooze for a few days, Miss Dorma?"

"I understood."

"You don't mind, do you? I think we'll feel safer with him around."

"John Michael will help us, for sure and for certain."

Already, Grace felt more at ease. With a burst of awareness, she realized that Dorma was helping her as much as she might have been helping Dorma. "I'm glad you're here."

"I like it here, too. I like you."

Grace felt the last of the tension in her shoulders ease. She had no idea what was going to happen next. All she did know was that the Lord had a plan. He must have one in order to put it all together.

Thinking of her new sense of peace and Dorma's improvements, she started talking, hoping that Dorma was understanding at least some of what she was attempting to convey. "You know, when I first realized I was going to be here while my family was gone, I was kind of sad. It made me realize that I had taken them for granted, too. I liked being around them, but I liked being by myself, too." She swallowed and forced herself to continue. "I'm embarrassed to tell you that I was kind of disappointed that they didn't argue too much when I said I had to stay behind."

After they stopped again so Snooze could take his time nudging a fallen pinecone with his nose, Grace continued. "But now I realize that the Lord wanted me to have these two weeks. He knew I needed to do some growing up."

"Have you grown up?"

"I think so," she said, realizing she truly had. "In ways I never imagined. I've thought about others instead of myself, I took risks, I've made mistakes, and I've learned new things. Because of that, I guess you could say that this has been a remarkable two weeks."

Dorma didn't say anything. Just kept walking by her side.

Grace figured that the right thing to do would be to simply be quiet, but she couldn't seem to stop. It was like she had so many words inside her, she needed to get them out. "You don't know this, but John Michael used to be my sister Beth's boyfriend."

"I knew that."

Grace felt her cheeks heat. "Now that I think about it, I would have been surprised if you didn't. They courted for several months."

"They seemed happy."

"Everyone thought so. My sister really liked him." She sighed. "*Nee*, Miss Dorma, it wasn't that simple. No, if I'm sharing this, I need to be completely honest. Beth loved him. We all thought that John Michael loved Beth, too. Maybe he did. But then, one evening, he came over and spoke with Beth alone. That's when he told her that he'd changed his mind."

"Ah."

She nodded. "Right in our living room, John Michael broke up with my sister. It was a shock."

"He didn't love her after all."

"I . . . well, I guess he didn't. She was upset and, I guess, surprised. All of us were. I think we were justified, though. Don't you?"

Dorma said nothing, merely smiled at Snooze, who was still walking happily. Leading them toward the mailbox.

"You know what's funny is that John Michael has never tried to excuse himself. He told me that he felt bad about not having the feelings for Beth that he wanted to have. He said the connection that he'd hoped to make just wasn't there."

Grace took a deep breath of the cold air, feeling like it was cleansing her from the inside out. "That's when I also realized that he'd moved on. He hadn't burdened himself with his worries or his faults. He had accepted them and also accepted the fact that in time both he and Beth would be glad he had broken things off.

That's when he started training to be a firefighter." She smiled at Dorma.

"He saved me."

"You're right," Grace said, feeling her way through the conversation. "Everything seemed to have happened for a reason. If he had stayed with Beth, he never would have felt the need to become a fireman. If he hadn't done that, he wouldn't have been there to help you."

"God is good."

"He is, indeed." Grace smiled, then continued. "It's hard to say it, but I think it was best for Beth, too. She's grown up a lot and become stronger. There's also been a certain blacksmith over in Indiana she met in Pinecraft. She's been keeping in touch with him. Maybe she was meant to be with this man."

Dorma looked at her. "Why have you been so confused, then?"

"Because my family has held on to that anger instead of letting it go, and it's done nothing but hurt us. We've needed to move on, to move forward. We need to learn to be happy."

Dorma looked at her and smiled. "Being happy is worth everything."

A lump formed in her throat as she contemplated those words. "You're right. It is worth everything." She focused on those words as she opened the mailbox and pulled out another stack of letters and catalogs. "The Lees sure get a lot of mail."

Snooze barked as if in agreement.

"Let's head back inside," Grace said. "Maybe when we get in, I could make us some lunch. Do you like potato soup?"

"I think I do," Dorma said. "I guess I'll know when I give it a try."

Grace had to laugh. That was the perfect answer.

# CHAPTER 30

It was four o'clock in the afternoon and John Michael felt like he hadn't slept in three days. As he looked around the day-room at the firehouse, he realized that the other men looked the same way.

"Is it usually this bad in December?" he asked, not really expecting an answer. "I don't remember it being so crazy last year."

"I don't think it was quite. But the weather was better," Sean said as he made himself a fresh cup of coffee in the kitchen nook.

"It wasn't as bad because it rained nonstop," Anderson said as he rooted around in one of the cabinets. "I'm half starving. Are these granola bars anyone's? Do y'all know?"

"I think a Girl Scout troop donated them last week," Hank said. "They're up for grabs. Take what you want."

"Perfect." Anderson grabbed two. "Anyway, all we had last year was rain instead of snow." Wrinkling his nose, he said, "There weren't as many car accidents, but everything I owned was coated in mud."

"My wife kept buying me more white undershirts and socks. She said my stuff was beyond bleach," Sean said.

"I remember the mud and the rain," John Michael said. "I just don't remember being so tired."

"You know what the answer to that is, John," said the captain, looking up from his bowl of chili. "We've got half a shift to go. If you're that tired, you need some sleep."

At another time, he might have felt like a kid being told to go to bed. But this time, John felt like his captain was right. Nothing was going to cure his problems besides a couple hours of shut-eye.

He stood up. "I'll see you all later. Hopefully much, much later."

"Get some sleep," Sean called out.

After grabbing a bottle of water, John went to his room for the night, pulled off his boots, and made sure the rest of his gear was also set out and easy to get on in seconds. Then he lay down, closed his eyes.

But, of course, now that he was trying to sleep, his mind started spinning . . .

The car accident they'd assisted at the beginning of their shift and what a blessing it was that no one had been seriously injured. Of Dorma, her fire, and how she'd lost so much but still seemed to be able to smile. But mostly he thought about Grace King.

He had come to terms with the fact that he loved her. She was the reason he'd waited—

Then he was awakened—

He'd been dreaming!

Dreaming of Grace and of Christmas . . . and a round of fire bells were now going off!

He didn't dare look at the clock, afraid it had been barely thirty minutes. Instead, he shoved his feet in his boots, grabbed the Swiss Army knife and a dozen other items he often stuffed in his pockets, and ran down the stairs.

Captain Butler was already in his turnout gear. "Hope you got some sleep, Miller," he said as he picked up his helmet. "We got ourselves another fire on the edge of the county."

"I'm feeling fine, sir." That was kind of a lie, but he figured it was close enough.

"Good to hear." He slapped him on the back before getting on his microphone again.

"Hey, Miller," Sean called out as John rushed to get into the back of the ladder truck.

"Yeah?" he said, attaching the SCBA and buckling in at the same time.

"Catch."

It was a Mountain Dew. *"Danke."* The men knew how much John enjoyed that particular soda, and that he tried not to have it too much. But that jolt of cold caffeine and sugar was absolutely what he needed.

"Just don't spill it," Hank grumbled. "If you spill it all over the insides of this truck, you're cleaning it all up by yourself."

"Understood."

As Hank pulled out and the lights flashed, John held on with one hand and took a deep swallow with his other. He was ready to go again.

Four gulps later, he was done. After setting it behind him so it would be out of the way, John Michael started doing what he did best. He started praying.

# CHAPTER 31

When the doorbell rang and Grace peered through the windows by the front door, she let out a cry as she pulled the door open wide.

"Mamm! You're back!" She rushed into her arms.

Grace's mother hugged her tightly. "Indeed we are, child. As soon as we unpacked, I hurried over here."

After lingering for a moment longer, Grace stepped far enough away to see her mother's face. She looked as she always did, like an older version of Beth. Her golden hair was lighter than it used to be, thanks to the addition of gray and white strands. There might have been more lines around her eyes than there were five or six years ago, too.

As always, what stood out to her was her *mamm*'s bright smile framed by the high cheekbones Grace had inherited. There had been so many times in her life when she'd looked to her mother's reassuring smile for comfort.

It had always been given freely.

"I'm so glad you came back early. I've really missed all of you."

"I promise, you aren't as glad as we are to be home."

Obviously, there was a story there. "What about Mommi and Dawdi?" she asked, belatedly looking out to the driveway for more people. "Did they come back here with you?"

"*Nee*," Mamm said as she closed the door behind her. Walking to the center of the entryway, she sighed. "As soon as they started feeling better, they began to fuss about the way Daed and I were doing things."

"They complained?" she asked as she led the way into the kitchen.

"Indeed, they did." Looking a bit amused, she added, "They complained about my cooking, the way the girls did laundry, about the boys being too noisy. Even about the way your father curried the horses."

"Oh, dear." She took her mother's cloak and bonnet and hung them on a brass coatrack near the back door. Then she started brewing them a fresh pot of coffee.

"They were a lesson in patience, for sure." Shaking her head in exasperation, she said, "I tell ya, there were a couple of times I thought your father was going to lose his temper."

"Daed?" Her father was known for being especially easy-going. "Uh-oh."

"They not only complained, they were not very gracious about accepting help, I'm afraid. We all started feeling like we were walking on pins and needles."

Grace had always thought her grandparents were rather particular about how they did things, but she was really sorry to hear they'd acted like that. "So even though you all went there to help them, you felt you had to leave?"

"It seemed like the best idea," she said with a smile. "Your little siblings were bored, your father was in a mood, and even my patience was getting stretched to the limit. It didn't seem very Christmasy."

"Were Mommi and Dawdi well enough to stay alone?" After she placed two mugs on the counter for their coffee, she walked toward the stove. She'd decided to make beef vegetable soup for Dorma that morning.

"I think so. Though I invited them, they wanted to stay home. It was for the best anyhow," Josephine said as she poured a cup of coffee. "They might have gotten sick again if they traveled such a long distance."

Picking up a spoon, Grace stirred the beef broth and then carefully added the vegetables she'd chopped just that morning. She was aware that her mother was watching her intently, no doubt making sure Grace was preparing the stew the way she'd been taught. "Well, I really am glad you came here to see me."

"Daed wanted to come with me, and so did Leona, but I thought it would be best if we talked, just the two of us."

Some of the joy she'd been feeling about the visit faded. "Ah."

"Go get yourself a cup of *kaffi*, dear. I'll help you with this." Before Grace could protest, Mamm walked to the sink, washed her hands, then started cutting up the meat on the butcher block. "I had a driver drop me off. She's going to pick me up in an hour."

Grace poured her coffee, then added cream and sugar. "You're only going to stay for an hour?"

"I need to help your sisters with the laundry and get the house organized. Now that we're going to be home for Christmas, there's much to do."

"Let me know if I can help."

Putting down the knife, Mamm turned to face her. "Come home with me now, Grace."

Feeling off guard, she shook her head. "Mamm, I canna do that."

"I think you should."

"I have responsibilities here."

"Dear, you can bring along whatever animal you are watching this week with you."

That's when Grace realized that she hadn't told her parents about Dorma or the fire or the fact that she was now looking after her. How could so much have happened in such a short amount of time?

"Mamm, there's something you need to hear. We need to talk."

"Which is why you need to come home. I need to fill you in on your grandparents and your little sister, too." She rolled her eyes. "Sylvia fancies herself in love with the boy living next door to your grandparents' house. She cried when we left, acting like her heart was breaking."

"Sylvia always feels like her heart is breaking. That isn't anything new."

"This might be different. And Beth, why, she is getting serious about Aaron."

"Aaron, who?"

"Aaron Yoder. They started talking around Thanksgiving."

Aaron was a blacksmith. He was handsome but quiet. She would have never thought he and Beth would suit. "I didn't know they were seriously courting."

"It's only been a month, but it's happening. The reason you weren't aware of it was because you've been so busy with all the animals you watch." She paused. "Among other things."

"Mamm. I'm sorry, but I can't leave the Lees' house right now. You see, there's someone I've gotten close to, and—"

Her *mamm* sighed. "You canna still be thinking about John Michael, are you? Because your father and I talked and we agreed that you shouldn't see him anymore."

Grace felt more than a little annoyed. Why was her mother trying to make her feel guilty about spending time with John Michael if Beth was seeing Aaron? "That's not how relationships work."

"It is in our family." She stared hard. "Do you hear what I'm saying?"

Oh, indeed she did! *"Jah."*

Grace realized her mother was acting like nothing had changed.

With a start, she realized that for Mamm, nothing had. She, on the other hand, had changed a lot. She'd grown up, become more independent, and maybe even more compassionate, too. She saw things differently now.

She also no longer had to have her mother's approval in order to do what was right. And speaking of right . . . she really needed to tell her about Dorma before she woke up from her nap and came downstairs.

Pulling out one of the kitchen barstools, Grace said, "Mother, we really do need to talk about something right now."

"You don't intend to come home with me, do you?" Some of the happiness that had been in her voice faded as she looked around the kitchen. "If it's not because of John Michael, is it because you've made yourself so comfortable in this place?"

Grace heard something new in her mother's voice. It didn't sound completely like criticism, but it didn't sound complimentary, either. "Not exactly. I do the best I can in the houses where I am working. You know that."

"*Jah*. But most houses aren't like this."

Snooze padded toward them, his brown eyes studying Mamm in a curious way.

Her mother smiled and knelt down. "Is this the *hund* you are watching?"

"It is. This is Snooze."

"You are adorable, pup." But when she leaned forward to grab him, Snooze jumped backward, like he thought she was going to hurt him.

Mamm gasped.

Snooze growled and then started frantically barking.

Her mother eyed him with disdain. "Is this how he's been acting this entire time?"

"Snooze takes some getting used to. He doesn't warm up to people easily."

"Your father ain't going to like it if he's barking at everyone in the house."

"I know that."

She got back to her feet. "Is that why you don't want to come home, because of this tiny terror?"

"I would have told you why ten minutes ago if you would have let me talk," Grace chided. "Every time I've tried to explain things from my point of view, you've interrupted me."

Her mother folded her arms over her chest. "Talk, then."

"There was a fire. Actually, there have been lots of fires in the area. It's been mighty scary. Most were of empty buildings and old barns, but Dorma Schultz's home burned down."

"Who?"

"Miss Dorma. She and her husband used to own all this land."

She shook her head. "I can't place her."

"Come on, Mamm. Remember how she used to give all the kids candy at church?"

"Well, I think I remember her now," she said in a vague way. "She was kind. So her *haus* burnt down? Well, that is mighty sad."

Now they were finally getting somewhere! "Yes it was."

"But I'm still confused. What does her *haus* burning have to do with you?"

"Grace?" Dorma called out. "Grace, where are you?"

Her mother's eyes widened. "Grace?"

Instead of answering, Grace walked toward the hallway. "I'm in the kitchen. My mother came to visit, Dorma. Come and say hello."

As they heard Dorma's soft footsteps approach, her mother walked to her side. "Grace, what is going on?" she whispered under her breath.

"I invited Dorma Schultz to live with me, Mamm."

"You invited her here?" Her voice rose. "To live with you in another family's home?"

Put so boldly, she knew it did sound presumptuous. "Well, yes."

Her mother closed her eyes in exasperation. "Grace . . ."

"Mamm, listen to me. Dorma has nothing. Not even any clothes. And it is Christmas. There was nowhere else she could stay."

"Grace, I'm sure there were other—" she began, just as Dorma peeked in. And like that, her demeanor changed. "Hello, Dorma. I'm Josephine King."

Dorma slowly approached, eyeing Grace's *mamm* like she was an unusual specimen at the fair. "Do I know you?"

"We've met before. I'm Grace's mother."

A beautiful smile transformed Dorma's usually lax features. She reached out and grasped Grace's hand and linked her fingers with her own. "Grace is a wonderful-*gut* girl. She has been a *gut* friend to me."

Though she at first looked taken aback, her mother nodded. "I am glad to hear that. Our Grace has a good heart."

Grace bent her head. That praise meant everything. *"Danke,* Mamm."

Still holding Grace's hand, Dorma squeezed it. "She is going to be such a good *frau* to John Michael. Ain't so?"

And just like that, all the warm feelings that had insulated her evaporated within seconds.

"A *gut* wife, daughter?" her mother asked in a chilly voice. "It seems we have something more to talk about."

Dropping her hand, Dorma looked around the kitchen. "Is John Michael here or is he still sleeping?"

"Sleeping? As in here?"

"It's not what you think, Mamm."

Her mother rubbed her temple. "Oh, Grace. I fear it is *everything* that I think."

Fearing that the discussion was going to get worse before it got better, Grace poured herself another cup of coffee. It was sure to be a very long conversation.

# CHAPTER 32

John was back at the firehouse washing fire trucks. Washing vehicles when it was below freezing outside was an unsung and underappreciated job. Though they closed the bay doors, the cold still seeped through. It became a race to wash and dry the vehicles before ice formed.

But now, as he stared at the engine, its red paint as shiny as if it had just rolled out of the factory doors, John Michael felt extremely satisfied. It was clean enough to eat off of, and they'd completed the job before another call came in or he got half frozen in the process.

"Looks good, Miller," Captain Butler said as he walked out of his office, Chief Nolan and Sheriff Brewer behind him.

"*Danke.*" He grinned. "To be honest, I always dread this chore, but I'm so pleased about it when it's done."

Chief Nolan chuckled. "I feel the same way about my paperwork."

John Michael smiled as he picked up one of the discarded cloths he'd been using to wipe down the sides of the truck, expecting the men to walk past him and into their vehicles.

Instead, they paused.

"Hey, John, come over here for a moment," Captain Butler said.

He tossed the used cloths on a table and looked at all three men expectantly.

"Is your girlfriend still housing Dorma Schultz?" Sheriff Brewer asked.

"Grace is living with her at the Lees' house. But she ain't my girlfriend. She's a just a good friend." Then, remembering the kiss they shared and how special it had been, he looked down at his boots. "I mean, yes, she is my girlfriend. Unofficially." Well, now he sounded like an awkward teenager.

His captain laughed. "We weren't trying to pry into your relationship, John. We just want to know how Miss Dorma is doing. Do you know? Has Grace said?"

"Well, I think she's doing okay. I mean, as well as can be expected, this soon after the fire. And, well, you saw how she was yourself. She's forgetful."

The sheriff stared at him intently. "Has she said anything more about the fire?"

John Michael wanted to look at his captain to get an idea of what he'd told the other men, but he didn't dare. He had a feeling that it was important that he speak for himself. "I don't think so. Speaking of anything to do with the fire upsets her, and Grace has been trying to calm her down, you know?"

"Has she mentioned her relatives to you? Given you any specific information about them?"

"*Nee.*" He swallowed. "I know that there are rumors that some of her relatives swindled her money from her. I've also heard that her two nephews had been after her to give them *more* money. She was afraid of them."

The fire chief and Sheriff Brewer exchanged glances. "She had good reason to be afraid of them," the sheriff said. "Yesterday we discovered some more information. Now we're fairly certain that they are the ones behind all the fires and the burglaries. My deputy found some of the items that were stolen in a pawnshop in Nashville. One of the workers mentioned Benjamin's name."

Feeling like things were finally turning in the right direction, John Michael smiled. "That's great news."

"It would be if they were in custody," Brewer replied.

"Are you looking for just the two of them, or for more people?" he asked before he realized he should probably keep his theory to himself. "I mean, that's a lot of work, setting fire to things and then robbing other houses."

"That's a good question. I think they have to have at least one more person helping them."

"What do you need me to do, Sheriff?"

"You're staying with Grace and Dorma now, aren't you?"

He felt his cheeks heat. "I am. So far, it's going all right. I'm glad I'm there."

"We're not your parents, son," Chief Nolan said with a smile. "Don't forget, I'm glad you are staying with Grace and Dorma."

"Sorry," he said, feeling even more embarrassed. "I guess I do sound like a worried teenager."

"How about I stop by tomorrow morning when you get off?" said the sheriff.

"It's fine. Whatever you need."

"Great. Hopefully, we'll have a quiet night."

"Yes, sir. Hopefully."

A few minutes later, when John was back upstairs in the day-room grabbing a bowl of soup, he went ahead and called the Lees' house. He wanted to check on Grace and Dorma and let Grace know the latest developments.

Unfortunately, she didn't pick up. He hoped she was out walking Snooze and that nothing was wrong.

Then the bells started ringing again and he didn't have time to do anything but race back downstairs, pull on his turnout gear, and climb into his jump seat.

"Shame we're about to dirty up this very clean truck, Miller," Hank said good-naturedly.

"It is a shame. A real shame, indeed."

FOUR HOURS LATER, pulling back into the garage, John Michael felt like he'd just been fighting a fire for forty hours instead of four. His arms and back were sore from handling the powerful hoses, his nose was running, his eyes burned, and the rest of him was covered with a thin layer of sweat.

He knew the other men felt much the same way. The three of them had climbed back in the truck like old men. The captain even grunted when he sat down in the passenger seat.

After the briefest of updates with Butler, John had leaned back in his seat. Hank drove the truck back, taking each curve with care, and smiling wearily at a little boy waving to him through his car window. John Michael kept to himself.

So had the captain. It was no wonder. They were all exhausted. The fire had run hotter and had acted more deadly than any of them had first imagined. The captain had ended up calling another team when the exposures—the buildings around the abandoned farmhouse—looked to be in danger of burning.

By the nature of the area, fighting the flames had been a dirty job. The frozen dirt had turned to mud from the heat of the flames—and that mud seemed to have remarkable suctioning abilities. There had been times when John Michael was sure that he was going to need a hand to pry a boot loose from the sludge.

Of course, the mud and dirt was now coating the clean truck.

Hopping down, John glared at the wheels. Those alone would likely take an hour to clean.

"Do you ever feel like we just fought a fire in the middle of a bog?" Hank drawled.

"I have." John lifted one mud-splattered leg. "Like today, for instance."

After Hank hung up his gear, he grabbed the hose they used for the vehicles. "How about I rinse everything off for a round, then you can follow and scrub?"

"You're going to help?"

"Yeah. There's no way I could leave this to you on your own."

"I appreciate it," John Michael said simply.

"Don't worry about it. We're all a part of the same team, right?"

He nodded, liking the reminder. They really were all on the same team—just as he was on the same team as Grace.

Now he just had to be sure that she stayed safe and secure and happy. He didn't ever want to let her go.

# CHAPTER 33

You don't have to make me breakfast, Grace," John Michael said. "I can go home or make my own."

Grace looked fondly at him, knowing that if she hadn't realized she was falling in love with John Michael before that moment, she would feel like she was when he said things like that. "It's no trouble. If I'm cooking for two, I might as well cook for three."

"All right, then. I'm afraid I don't have it in me to protest any more than that."

"You had a rough shift, didn't you?"

"*Jah.*"

"Would you like to talk about it?"

He rubbed a hand along his smooth cheek. "There's not that much to tell you, other than I cleaned the ladder truck from top to bottom twice."

"One day, will you take me over there and show me all the trucks and the equipment?"

"You'd want to do that?"

"Of course. It's not only important to you, but I want to have a picture in my mind when you tell me about ladder trucks and such." As she placed a plate of scrambled eggs and sausage in front of him, along with two biscuits and a dish of honey butter, she added, "If it's not too much trouble, I want to feel for myself what that turnout gear feels like."

"When things settle down I'll take you."

She smiled at him. "Eat up now."

"I want to wait for you."

"Dorma and I ate an hour ago."

"I guess it is late, heading toward nine. Practically the middle of the day for you, being an Amish girl."

She giggled. "It's not quite that, but Dorma and me have been up for some time. She likes to go along with Snooze and me on our morning walk."

"That's good for her." He spooned a bite of eggs into his mouth. "This is good, Grace. You make a fine breakfast."

"*Danke*." She turned from him and began slowly washing the dishes in the sink so he wouldn't feel obligated to eat slowly or try to make conversation.

But by the time he finished his plate, she had finished scrubbing all the pans.

When she held out a hand, he ignored it and took his plate to the sink. "I'll wash my dish."

"Suit yourself." As he focused on the small task, she knew it was time to bring up her mother's visit. But how did she broach the subject without adding a good bit of her frustration to the storytelling? The last thing she wanted to do was make things more uncomfortable than they were about to be.

When the faucet turned off, he spoke. "Hey, Grace, we're going to have visitors today."

"Oh, I know." Maybe he'd already heard about her mother?

"How did you hear?"

"I was just going to ask the same of you." She smiled. "Or are you not surprised that my parents came back early and they aren't real pleased that you are living here?"

He coughed. "*Nee*. I had no idea they were back."

"So you were talking about something else? What visitors were you speaking of?"

"The sheriff and the fire chief are going to be stopping by within the hour."

"Again?"

"They have some more questions to ask Dorma about her nephews." He frowned. "I'm sorry, Grace. I know you feel like there's nothing else to say. They're really desperate to find these guys, though."

"I sure wish you would've told me they were coming the minute you got home." She felt her cheeks heat. "I mean here."

"I know that, but I knew you would have fretted, and there wasn't anything you could do."

"I suppose you're right. Besides, I have some news for you, too."

"You mean about your parents?"

"My mother came over yesterday and she's mighty unhappy with me."

"Because of you and I?"

"Yes. And because I didn't want to leave here and go home. And because of Dorma. And because you're staying here."

He froze, then smiled slowly. "Hmm. I guess I could probably understand why she wouldn't have wanted to know I was sleeping here. Did you tell her about the robberies and the fires?"

"A little bit. But I didn't want to alarm her."

"Sounds like she might be alarmed anyway."

"It wasn't good. When she left, she made sure that I knew she wasn't happy with me."

"Did she say anything about Beth?"

"Only that Beth was going to be mad at me, too."

"What are you going to do?"

Grace liked that he asked that question instead of telling her how she should handle her family. "Nothing," she said after turning a couple of answers over in her mind. "I'm not going to abandon Dorma or Snooze or the Lees."

"Or me?"

"Or you." Though her face felt warm, she forced herself to be open and honest with him. "You make me feel safe, John. It may be selfish to admit it, but I don't want to leave just because my parents want me to make Beth's life easier."

"For the record, I think I would have done the same thing," John said.

"Really?"

He nodded. "Mr. and Mrs. Lee are going to be home soon, so it seems kind of silly to relocate now. And Dorma seems like she's doing so much better."

"She is. I feel certain she is."

"I know she's going to have to move somewhere soon," said John Michael, "but I think if you do that now, just when she has gotten settled, it might cause her harm."

"If I took Dorma to someone else's house, I'd feel like I abandoned her," Grace admitted.

"I'll support you with whatever you want to do, but be warned—you are going to have to live with the consequences."

"I'd rather live with consequences from something that I chose to do instead of something I was forced to do."

John Michael's expression filled with respect. "I like the sound of that."

Feeling like she'd just climbed over another hurdle, Grace smiled. "I think I like it, too."

He smiled back at her—

Just as the doorbell rang.

# CHAPTER 34

Sure that the chief and captain were outside, John Michael began thinking of how he could help them question Grace while trying to support her at the same time. But his preparing was stopped in its track.

John Michael got a shock when Grace opened the door.

Feeling as if he was in the middle of a terrible play, he greeted her when Grace opened the door. "Beth. Hello."

She looked as pretty as ever. Maybe even more so, thanks to the way the cool air had made her cheeks look rosy. Also new was the look of hesitation in her eyes. All the self-assuredness that he'd used to think went hand in hand with her was missing.

"John Michael," she said softly. "Hello, Grace."

Grace paused for a moment before hugging her sister tight. "Beth, it is so *gut* to see you."

John stepped to the side, watching the reunion with interest. Beth seemed to be as happy to see Grace . . . though, there did appear to be some tension.

When Grace pulled away, she bent down and scooped up the barking dachshund. "This is Snooze."

"The whole reason you came over here." Beth smiled and held out a hand for the dog to sniff. "He's cute."

"He is." Grace glanced over at him before visibly steeling her shoulders. "So I guess you came over to see for yourself all what Mamm reported."

"I did."

"I'm surprised she let you come over here alone."

"You should be. Everyone in the family wanted to come over."

Grace shivered. "That would have been horrible."

Beth glanced from John Michael to her sister and back again. "Can I come in? I thought we all should talk."

"I want to talk to you, too, but this isn't a good time," Grace said.

"Why is that? You two seem very homey and domestic."

"There's no need to make things more awkward than they already are, Beth," John said.

"I don't think my being here is making things worse," she retorted.

Grace pointed at the street behind her sister. "You aren't the reason we canna talk," she said. "They are."

Beth winced as she saw a pair of cars parking in the circular drive. "Why are all of those men here?"

"Because they think Dorma Schultz's relatives might have something to do with all the break-ins and the fires."

"What fires?"

"The fires that have been taking place on various Amish properties around the county," John Michael supplied.

"And the robberies that have been targeting Englisher homes like this one."

"And both of you are involved?"

"*Jah*," John Michael said.

"But not intentionally," Grace pointed out.

"I think I had better stay."

Grace groaned. "Beth, there's no reason to do that."

"I think there is. You're going to need as much support as you can get." Since they'd run out of time and there wasn't really anything that could be said in a moment, John stepped forward and welcomed the chief and Sheriff Brewer. "Come on in. We're all waiting for you."

He waved a hand. "This is Grace and her sister Beth. Grace, I believe you remember Sheriff Brewer? And this is Chief Nolan."

After all the rounds of introductions had been made and

Snooze had settled, Grace walked everyone into the living room. "I understand you have some questions for me?"

"Yes, but they involve Miss Dorma, too." Sheriff Brewer looked around. "Is she here?"

"She is upstairs," Grace said. "I'll go get her."

"I can do that," Beth said. "If you tell me where she is."

"*Danke*, but she might not want to come with you," Grace said. "Dorma doesn't trust too many people." Looking at the sheriff, Grace said, "I'll be right back."

When she left, Sheriff Brewer looked at John. "Have y'all seen any more suspicious activity? Footprints or the like?"

"Not a thing," John answered. "I'm hoping that's a good thing."

"We hope so, too," Sheriff Brewer said lightly as Dorma and Grace joined them.

After Dorma sat down next to Grace, Sheriff Brewer said, "Have you seen your nephews, Dorma? Samuel and Benjamin?"

She shook her head. "*Nee.*"

"Are you sure about that? This is important."

Dorma began to tremble. "I don't want to see them again."

"Why is that?"

Dorma glanced at Grace, who nodded and took hold of her hand. After a few seconds passed, she spoke again. "I don't want to see them because they scared me last time I saw them. And they took my money."

"Were they alone? Or maybe one of their friends was with them?"

"They were alone."

"Where's your *bruder*?" John Michael asked.

She shook her head in dismay. "I don't know. My husband is gone, too. I'm all alone now."

Grace inhaled sharply, then bit her lip. John could tell she was trying her best to keep her emotions under control, but it was obviously hard for her to do. He didn't blame her, either. It was difficult to watch Dorma get questioned—and see all the brightness and sense of ease fade from her face.

He feared that the questions weren't helping the case at all but were making Dorma's mental state far worse.

"I think we should stop," he said at last. "This is very upsetting."

After Dorma got up, saying she needed to go wash her face, Sheriff Brewer looked intently at Grace. "John Michael, I know you feel protective of Dorma and don't like seeing her upset, but I can't give up. There's too much at stake."

After darting a worried look down the hall, Grace spoke up. "Do you really think more properties around here are in danger?"

"I think so. They've been successful, so they're getting bolder. But more importantly, we think these characters might try to reach out to Miss Dorma again."

"But why? She can't help them."

"They see her as a ways to their means. They're hunting for money, and they might think she has some more hidden away."

"But she doesn't." Grace turned to Dorma, who was quietly walking back into the room. "You don't have any money hidden away, do you?"

She stopped. "Oh, *nee*," she said after thinking about it for a moment. "Only the money in my memory box."

Everyone looked at each other. "What is that?" Beth asked.

"It's a lovely wooden box made of polished cherry," Grace answered. "But it wouldn't be worth much to anyone but Dorma, I'm afraid." Smiling softly at the older lady, Grace said, "Your memory box holds letters from your husband, right?"

The older lady's eyes brightened. "*Jah*. I keep my Abraham's letters tucked inside. Letters and all the money hidden away."

John Michael swallowed a gasp of surprise.

"Did you say *money*, Miss Dorma?" Grace asked.

"Oh, *jah*. I've kept everything hidden away for safekeeping. Just like my husband told me to do."

While Grace turned to John Michael and stared, Sheriff Brewer leaned forward. "I think we need to see that box, Miss Dorma. I think it would be a real good idea."

# CHAPTER 35

It was getting close to five o'clock. Knowing that Beth needed to get on her way, Grace and John Michael walked her out to the front porch. It was cold outside. Too cold to linger, but that's what they did. It seemed none of them could stop talking about the events of the day.

Selfishly, Grace was glad that both her sister and John Michael were just as anxious to talk about things as she was. If she'd been alone, Grace was sure she would have worn a path into one of Mrs. Lee's expensive Persian rugs while she reviewed the conversations that had just taken place.

"I still can't wrap my head around it," John Michael said as he sat down on one of the wicker chairs on the porch. "How does someone keep a hundred thousand dollars in a box?"

"There was a cashier's check in there," Grace pointed out.

"*Jah*, but the rest was in one-hundred-dollar bills."

"There were so many of them," Beth said. "Lots and lots of them."

"All stuck neatly in envelopes," Grace added. She shook her head in wonder. "I thought Sheriff Brewer was going to fall off his chair!"

"I thought he would take it from her, and then we'd have a real crisis on our hands," John Michael said. "Miss Dorma really didn't like any of us touching those envelopes."

"At least Chief Nolan said he would come back to help talk to Miss Dorma again if we needed it. Somehow we've got to convince Dorma to put that money in the bank."

"Now everything her nephews have been doing makes sense. They've been looking for that money."

"But why burn her house?" Grace asked. "The money could have been burned as well."

"Maybe that fire was more of an accident than we previously thought. Maybe they were planning to scare her, but it got out of control," John Michael said. "Or they thought if Dorma lost her house, she'd be forced to uncover all that money so she could get a new place to live."

"And, actually, that kind of is what happened," Grace said. "Dorma got out the money after she lost her house."

Beth raised her hands to her temple. "I think I'm starting to get a headache just thinking about it. I can't believe we missed everything that's been going on, Grace."

"It has been a lot, but it's probably just as well. You were taking care of Mommi and Dawdi."

Beth gazed at them both. "All of us being gone also helped the two of you figure things out."

Grace felt like her heart was stopping. "Beth, I didn't mean to do anything behind your back."

"Grace, let me," John Michael said quietly. "Beth, your sister isn't to blame. It's me. I . . . well, I don't know how to explain what happened."

"Then maybe you should let me do that," Beth said quietly. "What happened was that the Lord knew that you and Grace were meant to be together, not you and me. He simply provided the right time and place and allowed you to at last act on those feelings."

"I never wanted to hurt you. When we were seeing each other, I thought we were doing the right thing."

"I know you did. I tried, too." Beth swallowed, then said, "Grace, not to embarrass you, but I knew you had a crush on John Michael."

She pressed her hands over her face. "Oh, Beth. I was only sixteen."

"I didn't take it seriously . . . but I would have had to be blind not to notice." Turning to John Michael, she said, "I would also be lying if I said I never noticed how close the two of you had become."

"We were close, but I would've never done anything. I was loyal to you, Beth," John Michael said as he got to his feet.

"I know you were loyal. And I know you would have never cheated on me with anyone while we were together." She sighed. "And between the three of us, after I stopped crying, I realized that while I was hurt, I was also embarrassed because I knew John Michael had done the right thing."

"But Mamm—"

"*Jah.* I love our mother dearly, but she enjoys being our champion sometimes a bit too much. I knew if I told tell her that I was secretly relieved that John Michael had ended things, she would have been beside herself. So I kept that to myself."

She shook her head. "It all ended for the best. Besides, I feel differently around Aaron. It feels right, and like the right time. I now know the difference, and I know that it was right to wait for God to show me who my match was." Looking at the two of them, she smiled. "Just like God has done that for you both."

Grace glanced at John Michael. He was standing stoically. Maybe he was shocked by Beth's revelations.

Maybe he simply didn't know what to do next.

But as Grace looked at Beth, saw the vulnerability etched in her face, saw the love in her eyes that no doubt mirrored her own, Grace knew what she needed to do.

She walked over to her sister and hugged her tightly. After a second's pause, Beth hugged her back.

"*Danke* for coming over, for saying what you did."

"It wasn't easy."

"I know it. And that's why it means so much. Thank you again."

"No need for that. It was past time," added Beth.

Grace could feel her sister's smile. That was all she needed to know that everything was going to be okay between them. Maybe not today or tomorrow, but eventually.

She only needed their relationship to be real and open again.

Pulling away from her, she whispered, "I don't want to hurt your feelings, but I should let you know that I think I've fallen in love with John Michael."

While Beth smiled, John Michael called out, "Grace, you know I can hear your conversation, *jah*?"

Meeting his gaze, she nodded. "Maybe it's easier for me to tell you like this."

When John Michael said nothing, only continued to stare at her closely, Grace feared that she'd just made a terrible mistake. She should have kept her thoughts to herself.

She certainly shouldn't have blurted out something so special and private right there with Beth looking on.

As the tension between them pulled and tightened, Beth laughed. "I think now would be a perfect time for me to finally head on home."

Grace forced herself to look away from John Michael. "What are you going to tell Mamm and Daed? Do you think they're going to ask you a lot of questions?"

"About you and John Michael?" She rolled her eyes. "Absolutely."

Grace could already picture them both arriving in the morning, full of good intentions and heavy-handed advice. "What are you going to tell them?"

Beth's expression softened. "I'm going to say that I've given you my blessing and, maybe, remind them of something as well."

"What is that?" Grace couldn't begin to guess.

"I'm going to remind them about how precarious everything's been here in Hart County this month, and how one mustn't take anything for granted . . . or shy away from happiness." Beth smiled. "Why would we want to look at you and John Michael falling in love as anything but a blessing?"

Grace reached for her hand. "You really believe that, don't you?"

"I do. When you're in love—really in love the way you two are? Everything else, well, I think it pales in comparison." She took a deep breath. "Now, if you don't mind, say a little prayer for me.

This conversation with our loving, nosey parents is going to be necessary, but I have a feeling it ain't going to be easy."

"I'll pray all night!"

After they hugged again, and Beth waved a hand at John Michael, she walked to the buggy and guided the horse back down the snow-covered drive.

# CHAPTER 36

When Beth's buggy disappeared, John Michael wrapped an arm around Grace's shoulders. "Let's get you inside, it's cold out."

She didn't say a word as he ushered her in, shut the door behind them, then led her into the kitchen.

He wished she would say something, because for the life of him, he couldn't figure out how she was feeling. Was she relieved about her sister's words? Embarrassed that she'd confessed so much?

Maybe worried that he hadn't poured his heart out to her sister, too?

He supposed the only thing to do was ask. "What's on your mind?"

She jerked around to face him, studied his face, then kind of smiled. "Oh, John Michael. What isn't?"

"Your answer ain't helping me much, Grace."

"What are you worried about?"

"Everything. What just happened, that conversation between us and Beth. Well, it had been a long time coming. To be honest, I didn't know if it ever was going to happen."

"I didn't think it would." Eyeing him carefully, she said, "I loved growing up with my sisters. Though I loved my brothers, too, I've always been far closer to Beth, Leona, and Sylvia. My mother read *Little Women* to us when we were small, and I loved the story. I felt like I was living the *Little Women* story life."

"I've never heard of that book."

"No, of course you haven't. It isn't something most Amish read.

It surely isn't something that boys ever read, I don't think." Nibbling on her bottom lip, she got a dreamy look on her face. "The book is about Jo, who wants to be a writer, and Amy and Beth and Meg. They were four sisters living during the Civil War. It was wonderful-*gut*."

"I guess so."

Her smile grew brighter. "Each of us always argued over who was who. Except for Beth, of course. She was always Beth in the book, even though Beth dies."

John Michael raised his eyebrows at that. Privately, he thought that he was glad that he'd never had to read such a thing, and secondly that he would have certainly tried to be someone besides the girl who died. "Um, not to sound like a man, but I don't understand why you brought it up."

"Oh! Well, because we are really close. There's a line somewhere in the book about how the bonds of sisterhood will always come first. And that's how I felt about my infatuation with you. I was embarrassed about how much I liked you and felt mighty awful that the first thing I thought of when I heard you broke things off was that you would be free for me." With a gasp, she slapped a hand over her mouth. "My word! Forget I said that."

"I don't know if that's possible."

"John Michael. Really. Try harder."

"How about this? How about I finally share something about you, too?"

"What is that?"

"That you aren't alone. I knew I was fond of you years ago. I knew you were trouble for my heart during these three years. I knew I could never resist you. But now I know that no matter what happens in the future, I will have fallen in love with you."

"Oh."

"Yeah. Oh." He couldn't help it; he grinned like a fool. "I aim to pay a visit to your father and ask for his blessing, Grace. I aim to marry you."

"Are you going to ask me?"

"Of course. I'm going to do it right, though. At the right time, and at the right place."

"Now seems like a good time and this is a beautiful room."

"It's a good time but not the right one."

She knew he was right, but she was anxious, too. "Do you think you'll know when the right time is?"

"Oh, for sure. We'll be safe, all this trouble will be simply a memory, and nothing will be on our minds but planning our future. That will be the right time."

"I hope such a time and day exists."

"It will. I can promise you that."

"You can make that promise?" asked Grace.

"Absolutely," he said in that confident way of his. "We've waited too long for it to be otherwise."

"It's getting late. We should probably go to bed soon," Grace said.

"How about you check on Dorma and I'll walk around and make sure everything is locked up tight?"

"The sheriff didn't exaggerate did he?" asked Grace.

"About the danger you've been in? *Nee.*"

"I hope I'm not making a terrible mistake by insisting on staying here."

"We don't know what Samuel and Benjamin are going to do. The sheriff doesn't know, either. We just have to trust that the sheriff and his deputies are doing their jobs, just like I'll do mine when I go back on duty."

She nodded as she walked up the stairs.

Everything felt so out of order and off-kilter. She never imagined that she'd be so bold. Or that John Michael would talk about marriage like it was a certainty . . . but then just as confidently relay that the timing wasn't right.

She also never would have thought that they would declare their love for each other, talk about marriage . . . and not even kiss again!

She was still dwelling on it all while she walked down the hall to Dorma's room.

Once again, her door was open. A dim ray of light was streaming into the hallway.

Thinking that Dorma had forgotten to turn off her flashlight, she walked in the room.

And found Dorma sitting on her bed, the precious box and the wealth of letters surrounding her.

"Dorma, I didn't realize you were still awake."

"I wanted to read my letters."

Grace sat on the side of the bed. "It's a blessing that you have them still. Rereading them must make you feel close to Mr. Schultz."

She picked up one, fingered some of the writing, then rested it on her lap. "I suppose it does. Sometimes it just makes me sad, though."

"You loved him and miss him."

"I do miss him." Gazing at Grace, she said, "Nothing is the same. I miss how things used to be."

"I'm sure you do."

"I am thankful to you for bringing me here."

"I meant what I said, I'm glad you are with me. I like your company. But you do know this isn't my house, right? One day we are going to have to move out of here."

"What will happen to me then?"

"You will go wherever I go."

Something in Dorma's eyes settled. Clarity returned and it was so sharp, it fairly took Grace's breath away. "You won't leave me? You won't abandon me?"

Grace didn't know what was going to happen next, but she did know that she wasn't about to forsake Dorma again. "I won't abandon you. As long as you want to live with me, you will. This I can promise you."

She blinked rapidly. "You're a kind woman, Grace."

"I'm only saying what's in my heart. That's all." She stood up. "Now, let's clean up these letters and put them away so you can get some sleep."

"I am tired all of the sudden."

After they gathered everything up and Dorma placed the letters back in the wooden box, Grace picked it up. "Where do you want this?"

She pointed to a spot on the floor next to the legs of the headboard. "There."

"Down on the floor? Truly?"

"I can get to it easily, and no one would ever think of me keeping something so special on the floor next to the wall."

"I guess they wouldn't at that."

After the box was safely put away, Grace turned off the flashlight and placed it on the bedside table. "Good night, Dorma. Sleep well. Remember . . . before we know it, it will be Christmas."

"And so it is."

Grace walked to her room down the hall, thinking of the beautiful conversation . . . and how her heart felt full to bursting.

No matter what happened in the future, she'd had this evening, and that counted for a lot.

# CHAPTER 37

As John Michael restlessly checked and double-checked his gear while Hank drove the ladder truck down the highway, he felt like all the training, all the sore muscles, the hardships, and the hours of the late-night studying had come down to this night.

Less than eight minutes earlier, the bells had rung through the station house. He'd run down the stairs to his bunker gear, and Captain Butler had placed a hand on his shoulder and calmly told him the terrible news. His house was on fire.

His hands had been shaking as he'd picked up his helmet and pulled on the hood. His head was in a frantic mess as he'd pulled on the straps of his SCBA gear and got into the jump seat.

And now, when he usually took time to pray, his mind was blank.

"Miller, are you going to be able to do this?" Captain Butler called out to him from the passenger seat. "Are you going to be able to stay focused on your job?"

"Yes, sir."

As Hank drove through an intersection, blowing his horn at two vehicles, the captain turned to face him again. "You sure about that? Because we're going to need a hundred percent from you."

"You'll have that." If it was the last thing he did, he was going to give everything he had to fight this fire.

He just hoped they'd get there in time.

What if they didn't? What if his parents were trapped? What if they couldn't get them out?

What if they were already injured?

What if they were already dead?

"I know what you're thinking, Miller," Hank said, almost laconically as he raced down the highway. "But don't do it."

"It's Christmas Eve. I know my parents are home. And they're older now. Anything could happen."

"Ha!" Hank exclaimed. "Did you hear yourself?"

"Hear me say what?"

"That anything can happen." After he mumbled something and blared the horn again, he continued. "Anything can happen. Sounds like the Lord helping us out on Christmas, don't you think?"

John Michael felt a little affronted. "Are you making fun of me?"

"Of course not. I'm saying we have to think positive. We have to believe in ourselves."

"John, you need to grasp ahold of your faith and hold on tight," the captain added.

"I can't seem to find it right now," he admitted.

"Then you better start praying," Hank said.

"I've been trying. My mind is blank."

"How about the Lord's prayer, then? I can help you say it." Without giving John Michael a moment to think, he boomed, *"Our Father. Who art in heaven . . ."*

To John's shock, the captain prayed into the microphone, as did Sean and Anderson, who were following behind them in the pumper truck. *"Hallowed be Thy name."*

Looking out the window, John Michael saw his house, saw bright orange flames shooting into the sky from the back of it.

His house was on fire—and even from this distance, he knew it was going to be difficult to save much of the place he'd always called home.

But instead of feeling despair and fear, he finally felt the Lord's will deep within him. A sense of peace surged through him as he at last joined in the familiar prayer. *"Thy kingdom come,"* he said, loud and clear. *"Thy will be done."*

The group of them continued together, their voices melding and calling up to heaven as one. John Michael had never felt the power of prayer more. Just as Hank pulled to a stop, John Michael said, *"Amen."*

The first sight of his house close-up nearly took his breath away. Almost half of it was wrapped in flames, and the heat that it was producing felt intense, even from his position inside the truck.

But then, off to the side, he saw both of his parents. They'd gotten out. His mother was even holding one of the barn cats.

"You see them, Miller?" the captain said gruffly as the three of them jumped out of the truck and started pulling line.

"I do," he said, thankful.

"Then, do your job."

John Michael didn't need any more incentive. He zoned every-thing out except for Hank's directives, stayed by his side as they fought the fire with all they had for the next hour. Another truck and crew joined them and worked on saving the barn and the other outlying buildings.

As the flames died down and the majority of the danger had lessened, John Michael was aware that an ambulance had arrived and some EMTs were guiding his parents toward the vehicle, warm blankets already wrapped around them.

Thirty minutes after that, the captain gave the signal for them to shut down the hoses. Feeling both mentally and physically ex-hausted but also incredibly blessed, John detached his regulator and lifted his face mask. The cold night air felt like a soothing balm on his skin.

They'd done it. He felt a burst of pride as he realized that they'd done their jobs well. The fire was out, and they'd saved the barn—and all the animals in it.

Most of all, his parents were all right, too. He hadn't lost them.

At once, the knowledge of all he could have lost hit him hard. A lump formed in his throat. He closed his eyes and breathed through it. Said a fierce prayer of thanks.

"John Michael."

He turned, realizing that Captain Butler was standing by his side. "Sorry, Cap. I didn't mean to zone out. I'm fine." He held up the hose. "I'll finish folding—"

The captain shook his head, cutting him off. "It ain't that, son. It's . . . well, we just got the call. There's another robbery in progress."

"Boy, on Christmas Eve, too. Those guys have no shame, do they?"

"It's at the house closest to this one, John," he said slowly. "The sheriff is right now on the way to the Lees' house."

The ramifications of what the captain was saying hit him like a back draft, nearly forcing him to his knees.

Grace and Dorma were completely alone.

"Captain, I'm sorry," he said in a rush. "I know you need me here, but I can't let them face this by themselves. Could you let my parents know I'll be back?"

"Of course." Captain Butler pointed to Chief Nolan who was waiting by his red SUV. "The chief is going to take you over there. Go. We've got this."

"Thanks," he said as he started running over to him.

He hoped they wouldn't be too late.

# CHAPTER 38

Snooze was howling. It was squeaky, loud, and sounded a bit like he was getting his paw chopped off.

Awakening with a start, Grace sat up in bed, peering around the room. She'd taken to opening the blinds slightly when she went to bed. She enjoyed seeing both the moonlight and the first rays of sunshine in the early morning.

Because of that, she didn't need to see the digital clock by the bedside. She knew it was right before dawn on Christmas Day. She also knew something was very wrong, because by this time of the early morning, Snooze was fast asleep next to her in bed. For him to still be downstairs by himself was unusual.

For him to be barking and carrying on? It made the hair on the back of her neck stand up.

Just as she rubbed sleep from her eyes, she heard a clank, as if something had just fallen off a table downstairs. When Snooze started barking frantically, Grace scrambled out of bed. The chill in the air kissed her skin, raising goose bumps. As quickly as she could, she slipped into the thick robe her mother had given her as an early Christmas present.

It was soft and cozy. Perfect to snuggle in on cold evenings. But terribly insufficient when it came to middle-of-the-night investigating. She wished she could take the time to get fully dressed. She was already feeling vulnerable. Investigating a disturbance in her nightclothes only made things worse.

Pulse racing, she opened her bedroom door and peered down

the long, narrow hallway. But it was all too dark; she couldn't see anything. Usually, she would have used a flashlight or simply turned on the overhead lights.

But something inside stopped her. Something was telling her that would be the wrong thing to do.

Especially since Snooze was growling now. Mighty loudly, too.

She took a hesitant step. She needed to help the dog, needed to see what was wrong . . . but was afraid of what she would find. If only John Michael wasn't working.

"What is going on?"

Grace squeaked and practically jumped a foot in the air. "Oh, Dorma," she gasped as she placed a hand on her chest and attempted to gather her breath. "You nearly scared the life out of me."

Dorma padded over in her thick robe and slippers. "You scared me, too. Snooze is barking."

"I heard him, too." As if on cue, Snooze erupted in another frantic round of yips, followed by a tiny, fierce howl.

Looking concerned, Dorma walked toward the steps.

Grace grabbed her arm, pulling her back into the shadows of the hallway. "*Nee*, Dorma. Wait."

"But Snooze wants us."

"*Jah*, but we need to wait," she said as quietly as she could.

"Why?"

Grace thought she knew why. Actually, it was pretty obvious. At last, after all the signs and all the warnings, they were getting robbed. "Bad men might be downstairs," she said at last. "I don't want you to get hurt."

Though the hallway was dark, Grace's eyes had adjusted enough for her to see Dorma shake her head.

"We should get John Michael," Dorma whispered.

She heard a loud clatter, followed by someone talking. Chill bumps raced up her spine as well as a deep, dark reminder that they shouldn't have been here in the first place. She could hardly count the number of people who'd told her to leave. But she'd been too stubborn and sure of herself to pay attention.

"Grace, we must get John Michael," Dorma repeated.

"We can't. He's working tonight." Suddenly, the obvious choice of what to do sank in. "Come on," she said, taking her hand. "There's a telephone in my bedroom."

When they heard Snooze bark and howl again, Grace thought Dorma was going to refuse, but she at last nodded and let Grace take her back down the hall. Once inside the room, Grace closed the door as softly as possible and dialed 911, explaining their situation to the dispatcher.

The woman on the phone promised help would be there soon, but warned them to stay upstairs and wait quietly until the sheriff arrived.

As soon as she hung up, Grace turned to Dorma. "Help is on the way," she said, wishing she felt as confident as she was trying to sound. "All we have to do it stay put for a little while longer."

Through the closed door, they heard poor Snooze bark again shrilly before crying out in pain. Grace's heart began to pound. Poor Snooze! He'd been hurt! He was probably so scared, too.

Dorma walked over to the door. "Snooze is downstairs alone, Grace!" she said as if just hearing him for the first time.

Grace hated that she was letting him down, but knew she had no choice. Keeping her voice firm, she said, "I know. He's doing a good job defending the house. But we canna go downstairs."

Dorma wouldn't listen. She turned the doorknob.

"Miss Dorma, *nee!*" Grace rushed to her side and stopped her. "You must listen to me. I know what you want to do, same as me. We want to run downstairs and help Snooze. But we can't. It's just me and you here. The robbers could have a gun. We could get hurt."

Dorma pulled on her arm but didn't try to open the door farther. When they heard a cabinet open, followed by the rustling of movement, she hung her head. Never had she felt so hopeless. Robbers were looting the Lees' beautiful house. Sweet little Snooze was in danger and probably wondering why no one was coming when he was trying so hard to get their attention.

This was all her fault, too. She should have left. She shouldn't have acted so brave and invincible. She should have listened to everyone instead of being so stubborn. Now everything she had hoped she could stop was happening. Leaving them all in danger.

"Miss Dorma, I'm so sorry."

"For what?"

"Everything."

As they heard more heavy footsteps and Snooze crying out again, the tears that had formed in her eyes began to fall.

"Are you crying?"

"*Jah.*"

After studying her for a moment, Dorma touched her arm. "Faith, Grace," she said softly, sounding more lucid than ever.

She hated to admit it, but she wasn't feeling much faith at all. All she had was a horrible sense of failure mixed with fear. "Dorma, if we hear the men come upstairs, I want you to go hide in the bathroom."

"*Got* will help us. You shouldn't worry."

Dorma was right, the Lord had helped her time and again. But even though Grace's faith was strong, she felt herself begin to have doubts. Bad things happened to even the most fervent of believers. After all, He didn't promise any of them an easy life— only one filled with the promise of heaven.

"Is it Christmas now?"

The question caught her so much by surprise, she almost laughed. "Oh my stars, Miss Dorma. You are exactly right. It is Christmas."

"Miracles happen on Christmas Day," Dorma said positively. "They'll happen for us now."

She wiped the new rush of tears that had slipped down her cheeks. "I hope so."

Dorma shook her head. "*Nee,* Grace. You must believe." And then, right as Grace was struggling to answer that, Dorma opened the door and walked into the hall.

"Dorma, stop!" she hissed.

"Who's up there?"

The voice sounded gruff and mean. Threatening.

"I am," Dorma said, clear as day.

Snooze started barking frantically at the sound of Dorma's voice. Which, unfortunately, encouraged Dorma to run down the stairs to him. Grace followed, more afraid than she could remember being during her entire life.

Dorma had been right. There was nothing better to do than pray.

"Please God," she whispered frantically. "Please help us." She had no time to come up with anything more coherent than that. Just as Grace reached the main floor, Dorma cried out . . . then rushed across the entryway, into the living room . . . and toward two men who were clad in jeans and T-shirts, and wearing gloves.

"Dorma, *nee.* Wait!"

But Dorma didn't wait. Instead, she reached out to the men with a pleased smile. "Samuel! Benjamin! You came for Christmas!"

Time seemed to stop as the men gaped at Dorma, Snooze hurried up to Grace's side, and the sudden, sharp sound of sirens broke through the air.

The sound was so welcome, it felt like Christmas had come at last.

# CHAPTER 39

Dorma, *nee*," Grace called out as she rushed to her side. "Come stand by me."

But Dorma wasn't paying a lick of attention to her. Instead, she was focused completely on the two men, men who were Dorma's nephews.

"Did you come to see me for Christmas?" Dorma asked again, trying to hug the pair. She was obviously unaware of the sirens outside, the tension in the air, or the danger the men posed.

Grace tensed, afraid that one of the young men would push Dorma roughly aside. But instead, the youngest one only pulled away from her grasp.

"Why are you here, Aunt Dorma?"

"I'm living here with Grace." The words were barely out of her mouth when the door was thrown open and Sheriff Brewer and Deputy Beck ran inside, their guns drawn.

"Hands up where I can see them!" one of them called out.

"Get down, Dorma," the boy said, pushing her toward the floor before doing as he was bid.

As Dorma fell to her hands and knees, and the sheriff yelled again, Grace crawled over to the older woman, holding her tightly.

The next few minutes fell into a blur. More uniformed officers came inside, and Dorma's nephews were handcuffed and pulled to the side, where Deputy Beck was barking questions at them.

A female officer guided Dorma and Grace, who was holding

Snooze, to the kitchen. She helped them sit down, got them hot tea, then asked them to share the events of the evening.

Grace did as best she could, but she was rattled and exhausted. She was also worried about Snooze. He didn't look to be injured, but he was shaking like a leaf and didn't want to leave her lap.

She also wanted to know what else was going on in the living room.

Never had she wished more that John Michael was nearby. Surely, he could get some answers!

Then, as if John heard her call, he walked into the kitchen. He was wearing a long-sleeved blue T-shirt on his top half and his firemen's pants and boots on the bottom half. He also smelled smoky.

Had he been in danger, too, tonight? Overwhelmed with relief, she got to her feet and ran to him. "John Michael!"

"Grace." He roughly pulled her into his arms, and she clung to him gratefully, not even caring who was watching them. "Are you all right?" he whispered. "They didn't harm ya, did they?"

"I'm fine. The sheriff came just in time."

After hugging her close again, he released her. Smiling down at her, he said, "I'll be saying prayers of thanks for that for the rest of my life."

"I think I will, too." Reaching out, she fingered the fabric of his pants. "You've been out fighting a fire."

His expression changed. "I have. They set my house on fire, Grace."

"What?" Just when she thought she had no more tears, they came again. "What about your parents? Are they okay?"

"Yeah. They're fine. We got there in time."

The female police officer stood up. "I think we have everything we need for now. I'm glad you're all okay."

"Me, too," Grace said with a watery smile.

When the three of them were alone, Dorma whispered, "The Lord kept his promises. He helped us get through the fire."

"Amen to that," John Michael said before gathering Grace into his arms once again.

WHAT AN UNUSUAL and wonderful Christmas morning, Grace reflected as she was looking around the Lees' ornate dining room table. Each chair was filled with people she loved—her whole family, Dorma, John Michael, and his parents, too. Her heart felt full to bursting with her blessings.

"I think we should have orange French toast every Christmas morning, Grace," her mother said as she placed another plate in the center of the table. "It's *wonderbaar.*"

"It is *gut,* but I think every meal is now going to taste especially sweet," John Michael said.

"I was thinking that very same thing," Grace's *daed* said to her. "Matter of fact, I don't think I'm going to be able to take my eyes off of you all day."

John Michael's mother squeezed her son's hand. "I feel much the same way. Last night was the most frightening of my life, but this morning has reminded me of how many blessings I've been given."

"Houses can be rebuilt and things can be replaced," Mr. Miller said. "We are just fine, and the animals are, too. Nothing else really matters."

Grace couldn't have agreed more. Soon after John Michael had arrived, the sheriff left with Dorma's nephews. And one of the deputies went over to John Michael's house, promising he'd bring his parents over to the Lees'.

When they arrived, they'd talked for several hours while John Michael and his parents took turns showering. All of them shared their stories. Then, after helping Mr. and Mrs. Miller into an empty guest room, Grace fell into an exhausted slumber.

Her family's arrival early that morning, just minutes after Grace had walked into the kitchen to start a pot of coffee, was a welcome surprise.

Her mother and sisters began fixing breakfast while Grace got dressed and took care of Snooze.

Now all of them were seated around the table, eating French toast and reflecting on the events that had transpired the night before.

"You two sure did good work last night," Grace's father said to her and Dorma.

Grace shook her head. "Daed, I can't say that we did anything much. We mainly hid."

"But you did call the police. That was good."

"I shouldn't have insisted me and Dorma stay here in the first place," Grace admitted. "If we had left, I wouldn't have put Dorma and Snooze in danger. I let my pride and stubbornness overrule good judgment."

"Not so fast," John Michael said. "While I would have loved to have known you were safe from harm, if you hadn't been here, those men wouldn't have been caught. Because you and Dorma were here and kept your cool, the series of robberies and fires that the county has been experiencing has ended. Everyone in the county is going to sleep much better."

When her sisters and even her mother nodded, Grace felt her cheeks heat. She didn't know if she'd actually done the right thing or not. However, she was mighty glad that things had turned out the way they had. "I'm simply glad it's all over."

"We all are," Mrs. Miller said with a smile. "I'm proud of you and Dorma." Looking at her son, her smile turned brighter. "And I couldn't be more thankful to have a firefighter son."

Beth raised her cup of coffee. "What matters now is that we've all remembered what was important and that we're all together, too."

"And that it's Christmas," Grace's sister Sylvia called out.

Grace raised her cup. "Here's to that. Merry Christmas, everyone! Cheers!"

Just as the rest of them raised their cups, the front door opened. And in came Mr. and Mrs. Lee.

"Grace?" Cindy Lee called out. "What is going on? There are two buggies out front. Tire tracks all over our lawn. What . . ." Her voice drifted off as she took in the scene in front of her.

While Snooze ran toward Cindy and Parker Lee, Grace jumped to her feet. "Um, good morning," she said hesitantly. "I'm afraid I have something to tell you. Things around here have been mighty exciting."

"It looks like you've decided to have a party," Parker Lee said.

While Grace swallowed hard, wondering how in the world she was ever going to share what had happened, her mother walked over to Cindy and Parker.

"I made French toast. We have orange juice, brown-sugar bacon, and coffee, too. Come join us."

Neither of them moved. Finally, Cindy found her voice. "I would rather hear what is going on."

"Yes!" Mamm said brightly. "Now come sit down and we'll all tell you everything."

John's mother shifted around the chairs. "You'd best do as Josephine is suggesting," she said to the Lees. "I promise, you're going to need some sustenance, too. It's quite the story."

# CHAPTER 40

"Well, you made it," John Michael said to Grace as they walked along the driveway in front of the mobile home his family was living in while they rebuilt their house. "You survived Christmas."

Grace looked at him and giggled. It was one week after Christmas and everything almost felt peaceful. She'd moved back home and helped Dorma get settled in their guestroom. John Michael and his parents had ordered a mobile home and already met with an architect about plans for the new house.

The Lees had not only forgiven Grace for inviting so many people to stay in their home, they called her their hero. They sent her family a giant fruit basket and had even given Grace a bonus as their way of thanking her.

And while Beth and John Michael still might never be good friends, they'd held fast to their earlier promise to put the past behind them.

Grace felt like she and John Michael were getting closer every day, doing things like they were doing now—simply walking outside and spending time together.

And teasing each other some, just like they used to do when they'd first met.

"You're right," she said at last. "I did survive Christmas, but barely! Just about everything that could have happened did. Fires, robberies, bad nephews . . ."

"Too many houseguests, runaway dogs . . ."

"And you," she finished with a giggle.

He pressed his hand to his heart. "Don't tell me you're going to place me in the same category as all those catastrophes."

"Of course not. You were the bright spot in the midst of everything." Then, as she thought of all the amazing things that the Lord had brought to her, she corrected herself. "Actually, now that I think about it, there were many bright spots in the midst of all the hardship and confusion."

He clasped her hand. Threaded their fingers together before bringing her hand to his mouth to kiss. "I've often seen that happen. Right when everything feels like it's never going to be okay again, something wonderful happens. Like finding you in the woods."

"Or when Snooze helped Dorma and me when Samuel and Benjamin broke into the Lees' house," she reflected. "Or, when you and I learned that there was so much more between us than we'd ever thought."

"Especially that."

NOW THAT SHE was home and sitting next to John Michael, it was even easier to catch the bright gifts that all the chaos had brought: her new relationship with Dorma, a newfound appreciation for her family, and even a fondness for one tiny, fierce dachshund.

"Snooze might have been my toughest client in years, but I'm sure going to miss him."

"I bet. You and him have been through a lot."

"We have. But so has everyone else. All of us in the county are going to have to come together to help the families affected by the robberies and the fires."

"And that was just this month! Think about everything that's happened in just the Amish community over the last two years."

Grace shivered. "There have been so many terrible things, from stalkers to women getting attacked to that awful incident over on the lake."

"Don't forget when that couple got stuck in Horse Cave. Or

when people were getting sick from that hidden still." John Michael exhaled. "I hope I am bored silly next year, though I have a feeling that won't happen. Here in Hart County, anything can happen."

"And it probably will." After sharing another tender look with him, Grace moved into his arms. Loving how secure she felt next to him, she continued. "What is most amazing to me is that after each one of those events, everyone who was affected became stronger."

John Michael hugged her close and brushed his lips against her cheek before releasing her. "The Lord has been answering so many of our prayers." Taking her hands in his, he said, "When a person feels like he isn't alone, he can feel like he can do anything."

"I know He's answered many of my prayers lately." Lifting her chin to gaze into his eyes, she confided, "Mere minutes before we reunited, before Snooze ran off after that squirrel, I'd been praying hard, asking the Lord to help me get through Christmas. I was afraid of being all alone. I certainly wasn't!"

After chuckling softly at her quip, John Michael turned serious. "Grace, I don't want to be without you again."

"I don't want to be without you, either."

He pressed his lips to her temple. "I love you. I know you love me . . . I don't want to wait any longer."

"I don't want to wait longer, either."

He paused, then reached for both of her hands. "Say you'll be mine, Grace King. Say you'll let me love you and you'll love me back for the rest of our days. Say you'll marry me."

Grace searched his face. Saw earnestness there. Saw passion and bravery and everything she'd discovered in him, even though she had thought she had already known him so well.

Then she looked just beyond him and through the windows. At the rolling hills. At the woods. At the snow and the tracks from the deer and the faint lights she could see in the distance.

This moment was like a dozen they'd exchanged.

But even more perfect.

So she said the only thing she could. Smiling brightly, she nodded. "I promise all those things, John Michael Miller. I promise to love you and have your love and be your wife."

Then he stood, and with his two strong arms, John Michael picked her up and swung her in a circle as she laughed.

And she was fairly sure the sound echoed through the valley . . . and maybe all through the county and up into the heavens, too.

She hoped so. Such happiness was meant to be shared.

# Meet Shelley Shepard Gray

In many ways, my writing journey has been like my faith journey. I entered into both with a lot of hope and a bit of nervousness. You see, I didn't get baptized until I was in my twenties and didn't first get published until I was in my thirties. Some people might consider those events to have happened a little late in life. However, I feel certain that God knew each took place at exactly the right time for me.

To be honest, these days I rarely stop to think about my life before I was a Christian or a writer. I simply wake up, drink my coffee, and try to get everything done that I can each day! I feel blessed to be a part of a large church family and a busy career. But, every so often, someone will ask why I write inspirational novels. Or why I write at all.

Then I remember how it felt to knock on a minister's office door and tell him that I wanted to be baptized. And how it felt the very first time I wrote "Chapter 1." Both felt exhilarating and nerve-wracking.

Perhaps you are a little bit like me. Maybe you, also, developed your faith a little after some of your friends or family. Maybe you, also, began a new job in a field that you didn't go to school for. Maybe you started on a journey where you weren't even sure you were going to be a success or even fit in.

Or maybe, like me, success wasn't what you were hoping to attain. Maybe it was a matter of following a power bigger than yourself. If so, I'm glad I'm in good company. I'd love to know your story, too.

Now I have been a Christian for almost thirty years. I've been a published writer for about half that time. Both journeys have not always been easy. Both have been filled with ups and downs. Yet both have given me much joy, too. I'd like to think that anything worth having takes some hard work. It takes some time to grow and mature, too.

And because of that, I am comfortable with the fact that I'm still on my journey, one morning at a time.

# Letter from the Author

Dear Reader,

Merry Christmas! I hope you enjoyed *His Promise*, as well as the entire Amish of Hart County series. Christmas books are my favorite novels to write, and this book was no exception, probably because it starred a very spunky dachshund named Snooze.

Do you have a pet? I grew up with dogs, and when our children were four and six years old, we got our first dog for them. Phoebe was an adorable beagle who ended up sleeping on the end of our son's bed for twelve years of her life. I think she missed Arthur as much as I did when he went off to college!

When Phoebe was about eight, we got Suzy, our first dachshund. Phoebe was doubtful about being around the spunky little dog at first, but they soon became best friends. Since then, we've adopted two more dachshunds, and a beagle-dachshund mix named Eddie. What's been gratifying for me is that we've passed on our love of dogs to our children. Each of them now has two dogs of their own. I guess the tradition has continued!

All these dogs make for a chaotic, messy, and loud Christmas. Ornaments have been chewed, presents investigated, cookies stolen from tables—and, yes, once Phoebe ate a whole pizza on Christmas Eve.

Other than the pizza episode, I have to admit that I kind of like the way our dogs have made our holidays so special. Our pets have given us so much joy and love. In a lot of ways, they've made our house into a home.

I hope you have a lovely Christmas season whether you, like me, have a houseful of canines or a houseful of friends and family. What matters the most is Jesus's birth and time spent with people you love. Thank you for making this book a part of your Christmas season, too!

Wishing you joy and peace and His blessings,
*Shelley Shepard Gray*

# Questions for Discussion

1. I thought the following verse from Psalm 9 was perfect for this Christmas novel. How does your faith fill you with joy? *"I will be filled with joy because of You. I will sing praises to your name, O Most High."*

2. I discovered the Amish proverb "Prayers go up, Blessings come down" after I finished the novel. I thought it was fitting since prayer helped many characters throughout the novel. When has prayer led to blessings in your life?

3. What did you think of Grace's original desire to have more of a "simple" Christmas? What are some things you do in order to remember the true meaning of the holiday?

4. One of my favorite relationships in the novel was Grace's bond with Dorma. Though Grace began seeing herself as Dorma's caretaker, she soon learned that Dorma was also taking care of her. Why do you think they needed each other so much?

5. I learned so much about firefighting, and about Amish firefighters, for this novel. What did you think about having an Amish hero with an unusual occupation? How do you think his faith helped make him a better firefighter?

6. What did you enjoy about Grace and John Michael's relationship? What do they have that John Michael had found to be missing with Beth?

7. Grace learns throughout the novel just how much she values her family and wishes she conveyed that more often. Is there anyone in your life that you feel you might take for granted from time to time?

8. I was so excited to have a dachshund as one of the main characters in the book. I based Snooze's character on two of our dachshunds, one of whom sleeps all day long. If you own a pet, how has it enriched your life?

# CRANBERRY SALAD

*1 can Eagle Brand Sweetened Condensed Milk*
*1 20 oz. can crushed pineapple*
*1 14 oz. can whole berry cranberry sauce*
*¼ cup lemon juice*
*1 9 oz. container of Cool Whip*

Mix all together and freeze in a 9-x-13-inch pan. Top with a ½ cup chopped pecans or walnuts, if desired, and serve.

Taken from *Country Blessings Cookbook* by Clara Coblentz. Used with permission of the Shrock's Homestead, 9943 Copperhead Rd. N.W., Sugarcreek, OH 44681

# CHERRY CHOCOLATE CHRISTMAS COOKIES

2 ½ cups butter, softened

4 cups sugar

4 eggs

4 teaspoons vanilla extract

4 cups flour

2 teaspoons baking soda

1 ½ cups baking cocoa

1 teaspoon salt

1 cup chocolate chips

1 jar maraschino cherries, cherries drained and halved

Preheat oven to 350 degrees. Cream butter and sugar until light and fluffy. Gradually add eggs one at a time, beating well after each addition. Add vanilla. Combine dry ingredients. Gradually add to creamed mixture. Stir in chocolate chips.

Drop by teaspoonfuls on ungreased cookie sheet. Bake approximately 8–10 minutes. When cookies are half baked, take out and place half a cherry on top, and then continue to bake until done.

*Tip~ a melon baller helps make perfect-sized cookie-dough scoops.

Taken from *Country Blessings Cookbook* by Clara Coblentz. Used with permission of the Shrock's Homestead, 9943 Copperhead Rd. N.W., Sugarcreek, OH 4468

# COCONUT PECAN BARS

*1 cup butter, softened*
*2 cups packed brown sugar*
*2 eggs*
*2 teaspoons vanilla extract*
*2 cups flour*
*1 teaspoon salt*
*1 teaspoon baking powder*
*1 ½ cups flaked coconut*
*1 cup chopped pecans*
*confectioners' sugar*

Preheat oven to 350 degrees. Cream the butter and brown sugar until light and fluffy. Adds eggs, one at a time, beating well after each egg. Add vanilla. Combine flour, salt, and baking powder, gradually adding to creamed mixture. Sir in coconut and pecans. Batter will be thick.

Spread in a greased 15-x-10-x-1-inch baking pan and bake for 20–25 minutes or until toothpick inserted near the center comes out clean. Cool, and dust with confectioners' sugar. Cut into bars.

Taken from *Country Blessings Cookbook* by Clara Coblentz. Used with permission of the Shrock's Homestead, 9943 Copperhead Rd. N.W., Sugarcreek, OH 44681